Acknowledgements

*One of my favorite parts of writing these Pauline Gray
novellas is depicting the warmth and community
of the small town she calls home. A book needs a
community, as well, and this one could not have made
it to publication without mine. A.M. Offenwanger
provided beta reading in the early drafts as well as
copy editing for the final stages. Any errors that remain
are mine, not hers. Samantha Johnson also beta read
this story, and I am grateful as well for her continued
championing of Pauline's stories. My dad, Kevin Bates,
is an invaluable resource for stories from "the old days"
in Canton, Clayton, and the surrounding areas. My
husband Carl has supported me through this book
as well as all my others; I would not be able to pursue
this writing career without his encouragement.*

CONTENTS

DIAMONDS TO DUST

By Louise Bates

StarDance Press

CHAPTER ONE

A Peculiar Legacy

Pauline Gray would rather have spent this March morning working on her newest Emma Daring manuscript, but the telephone call from Ruby Richardson, asking if she could meet with Arabella Warren, had intrigued her. She was just putting the final scoop of coffee in the percolator when the knock came at the door.

On her way though the living room to answer the knock, out of habit Pauline checked her desk. Yes, she had hidden the novel pages under the stack of books and inserted the half-typed page for her newspaper column in the typewriter instead. Nothing there to indicate that Miss Gray, newspaper columnist and St. Lawrence University graduate, wrote adventure novels on the side.

"Oh, hello," the woman at the door said in a gasp.

Pauline wondered what right the woman had to sound so surprised. If you knock at a person's door, you ought to expect them to answer.

Then again, Pauline thought, looking at the narrow steps that wound up the outside of the building to her second-floor apartment, perhaps the woman was merely breathless from the climb. Pauline did it so frequently she often forgot how strenuous the stairs could be if one wasn't accustomed to them.

"Hello," she answered, her voice revealing none of her thoughts.

Its very calmness seemed to reassure the woman, who blinked her large, pale blue eyes several times and gave a little sigh, seemingly of relief.

"Are you—you are Pauline Gray, the newspaper woman, aren't you?"

"Yes," Pauline said. "Are you Arabella Warren?"

"Yes—oh good, Mrs. Richardson told you about me. She said she had, but I—well, there. You already know all about it."

In truth, Pauline did not. Had Ruby not mentioned a problem, she would have supposed Miss Warren wanted her to run a piece in her column on something or other—a social function she was organizing, or a grandfather turning 100, something of that sort. Pauline did get those sort of requests from time to time. Occasionally her editors at the *Watertown Daily Times* even let her write them.

"Won't you come in and tell me about it?" she said now. "Mrs. Richardson only said that something odd had happened to you, and she recommended you bring it to me. I haven't heard any details."

"Yes, it is odd," Miss Warren said, following

Pauline inside the apartment and then standing irresolutely in the tiny entryway. "I don't know what to make of it, and I didn't know who to go to. It's not a police matter, so Mrs. Richardson told me when I asked her about it, nothing so serious."

Ruby was married to James Richardson, a lieutenant with the Canton Police Department.

"I haven't got a husband or brother or anyone to advise me, either," Miss Warren continued. "I don't dare go to the lawyers, they talk so much and use so many fancy words I can't understand them half the time—though it was a lawyer who brought the news to me, and he seemed like a nice enough fellow. But then Mrs. Richardson said, well, why not try that nice Miss Gray, she has those newspaper contacts and she has a knack for figuring tricky puzzles out, so well, here I am."

Pauline found herself tempted to do some blinking of her own. She was half inclined to send the woman on her way to save herself the bother of trying to unravel why she was here, much less whatever puzzle she had that needed solving, but Ruby had trusted her with Miss Warren's dilemma and she hated to let her friend down.

Besides, her interest was piqued.

"The coffee should be just about ready," she said. "Do let me take your things, and we can discuss this matter while we share a cup."

Miss Warren sighed again. "That is kind of you, Miss Gray. I'm that flummoxed I don't know what to do with myself. And it's a chilly morning to be walking across town, no doubt about it. A cup of coffee would be just the ticket."

Pauline took her hat, an unadorned grey felt with a deep crown and narrow brim, a style fashionable a few years back but not much in vogue this past winter. It was exquisitely neat and clean, indicating the wearer cared more for the quality of her wardrobe than the style.

The gloves Miss Warren handed her next confirmed this. The cotton lisle material and plain design were not particularly fashionable, but where they had worn through at one or two of the fingers Miss Warren had darned them so neatly as to be almost invisible. Pauline, whose darns always came out bunchy and looking worse than the original hole, felt a flash of admiration as she set hat and gloves on the carved walnut table in the hall and moved toward the kitchen.

She had expected Miss Warren to remain in the living room, as a proper guest, but to her mild alarm the woman followed her into the kitchen and sat right down at the square wooden two-person table. Pauline spared a moment to thank heavens she had washed the breakfast dishes and swept the linoleum floor before Ruby had telephoned. While she valued a clean environment as much as anyone, when deadlines loomed the housework did not always get discharged as promptly as she would prefer.

The floors weren't perhaps as gleaming as a diligent housewife would have had them, the counters not as spotless, but it was reasonably clean for an apartment shared by two working women, and Pauline put the matter out of her mind.

"Do you take milk or sugar, Miss Warren?"

"Oh—milk, if you have it. My father was a dairy farmer, you know, so we always had milk and cream around, no matter how short we were on anything else, and I grew up used to putting milk in everything. Not sugar so much, though, no, sugar was more of a treat. We used maple syrup generally for sweetening, but I don't take it in my coffee, good coffee is fine without any sweetener at all, don't you think? Even if I did prefer it, I would feel downright wicked wasting sugar in coffee when I think of how many people don't have enough food to keep from starving, poor things. It's a terrible world sometimes, Miss Gray."

Pauline pulled the milk bottle out of the tiny ice box without bothering to answer. Thus far Miss Warren was proving a fine contradiction: finicky in her dress and inconsequential in her speech; a woman of conscience but little gumption.

Her age appeared to be around forty; there was no grey in the blonde hair that frizzed about her round face, defying her attempts at smoothing it into finger waves, but she had laugh lines emanating from her faded blue eyes and an overall air of having lived through a good portion of her life already.

She removed her coat to reveal a light pink cotton dress which was, as Pauline half-expected, neat and tidy but a few years out of date; her low-heeled sensible shoes completed the pattern. In appearance, if not in speech, this was a competent, practical woman.

Pauline could think of no higher compliment to bestow on her fellow man—or woman.

"There," she said, handing a filled cup across the table to Miss Warren and sitting down across from her with her own cup. "I'm sorry I have nothing else to offer you, I am a terrible baker. Perhaps an apple ...?"

Miss Warren took a sip of her coffee. "No no, no thank you. I do so hate to ask people to feed me when we're all struggling to make ends meet. If I want food, I can prepare it for myself. No, this is fine. Thank you, Miss Gray. I suppose you want to hear what I've come about?"

"If you are ready to tell me," Pauline said with a smile.

The older woman drew in a steadying breath, drank some more coffee, then set the thick white cup down and interlaced her fingers around it.

"It's not a bad thing, not by any means. I ought, I suppose, to simply accept it and be happy. I mean, a diamond necklace ...! But it's so odd, and I can't help feeling nervous that there's some mistake, and well, I don't want to get mixed up in anything improper. You understand, I'm sure."

"I'm afraid not quite," Pauline said. "Perhaps if you went back to the beginning?"

"Of course. Well, I don't know where the beginning is exactly. If I did, I wouldn't be so muddled, would I? I suppose I should start with the lawyer. That's where it began for me, you see."

"Yes, the lawyer," Pauline said, gratefully seizing on this one concrete tidbit. "You mentioned him before. He brought you some news?"

"Yes, about the will."

"A will?"

"Yes, Mr. Van Camp's will. He left me something, you see."

"That was kind," Pauline said, feeling her way forward tentatively. "Did you know him well?"

Arabella Warren sat upright, pushing her hair back from her face. "No!" she said explosively. "I have no idea who the man is! I've never even heard his name before the lawyer showed up at my door this morning. According to Mr. Ramsey—that's the lawyer —Horace Van Camp was a wealthy man living in Clayton who died two weeks ago, but I don't know him from Adam."

Clayton was a small village on the St. Lawrence River, about fifty miles from Canton. It was part of the famed "Thousand Islands" region, the area of the river dotted with countless small islands that was considered one of the most beautiful parts of the state.

"Then why ..."

"Why should he leave me a diamond necklace in his will? That's what I want you to find out!"

Pauline sipped her coffee to cover her confusion. "I beg your pardon?" she said after she swallowed.

"Miss Gray, that lawyer man showed up on my doorstep to tell me someone I've never heard of died and left me a diamond necklace in his will, and I haven't the faintest idea why. Not that I wouldn't like a diamond necklace—who wouldn't?—but I don't want to accept something I shouldn't. What if he meant another Arabella Warren? Or what if there's some deeper mischief afoot? I don't like it—it makes me nervous—and I want to know more before I accept the necklace."

"Well," Pauline began.

"And that's why I came to you," Miss Warren carried on. Her knuckles were white around the coffee cup. Clearly the situation was more of a strain on her than Pauline would have expected.

Most people would be delighted with a mysterious bequest. They might puzzle over it a bit, but ultimately they would accept it and let the story become part of family lore.

Not Miss Warren.

"I asked Mrs. Richardson if her husband could look into it for me, and she said no, it wasn't a police matter, and that's when she said I should ask you. So here I am."

"What exactly are you asking of me?" Pauline said, searching for clarity.

"I want you to find out more about Mr. Horace Van Camp, who he was, who else he left things to in his will, and how he heard of me in the first place, not to mention why he would leave me a valuable necklace. I want you to come with me to the lawyer's tomorrow to get the necklace—he's holding it in his office for me to claim—so you can make sure it's all straightforward and aboveboard. I don't care if you make a story out of it for your paper, I just want to know the truth. Will you help me?"

Pauline considered it.

This woman seemed to have a keen mind under her rambling conversation, and judging by her attire, a love for order and neatness. A disorderly and puzzling affair such as this would affect her pleasure in the bequest and bother her every time she wore the necklace if it didn't clear up.

Pauline would have been the same in her place. She made up her mind.

"Miss Warren," she said. "I will."

CHAPTER TWO

Preliminary Investigations

After Miss Warren left, Pauline allowed herself the luxury of a second cup of coffee and sat back down at the table with it. A pleasant tingle filled her fingers and toes, the allurement of the unknown, a fresh puzzle to be solved.

Last fall she had gotten involved in a murder mystery. It hadn't been enjoyable, exactly, and some parts had been both appalling and terrifying, but the thrill of discovery combined with the knowledge that she was helping find justice for those unable to seek it for themselves had given her a sense of purpose and a deep-rooted contentment that she had missed in the months since.

On the face of it, this little mystery of Miss Warren's didn't seem as important as murder, but it was an exercise for her wits as well as a chance to help a neighbor in need. Pauline would not scorn either of those things.

She propped her chin on her hand and stared out the kitchen window at the bare treetops just starting to show hint of red at the tips of their branches. Why *would* a man leave a diamond necklace to a woman he'd never met? If Pauline were writing this in a novel, what would the reason be?

Clearly, because Arabella Warren was either his long-lost daughter or sister, depending on his age.

Pauline laughed and shook her head, then picked up her cup and finished her coffee. Alas, real life was rarely as uncomplicated or melodramatic as her adventure stories. Far more likely was Miss Warren's prosaic fear that he had meant to leave it to another Arabella Warren and it had come to this one by mistake.

Or perhaps he had been an acquaintance of her father or mother and wanted to leave their daughter a remembrance in his will. Perhaps he had heard of her or met her without her being aware of it and decided she was worthy of a diamond necklace. Perhaps she shared a name with a woman he had loved in his youth, and he wished to commemorate the lady.

She caught herself. There she was getting romantic again! Too much novel writing and not enough sound scholarship of late, that was her problem.

She wasn't going to get any answers sitting here thinking up less and less likely scenarios, and if she drank any more coffee she'd float away. The next step was to find out more about Mr. Horace Van Camp, and about Miss Arabella Warren herself.

Pauline washed the cups and spoons and dumped the coffee grounds out of the percolator into a bowl. Later she would take the bowl downstairs to her landlady, who used coffee grounds as a fertilizer for her prized roses.

The kitchen tidy enough to assuage her conscience, she pulled on a warm sweater, a pretty green cardigan knit for her by her favorite aunt as a Christmas gift. It had come with a matching beret, with Pauline now set at a jaunty angle atop her smooth dark hair. From habit, she tucked a notepad and freshly sharpened pencil into her handbag, and set out.

Emma Daring and her adventures would have to wait. Real life had become more exciting than the adventure novels Pauline wrote in secret to supplement her newspaper salary.

The March air was brisk but not unpleasant. The farmers insisted more snow was on the way, but today, with the sun shining and the pussy willows beckoning from the sides of the road, spring's promise was everywhere.

Pauline was thankful. Goodness knew that anyone who chose to live in northern New York state had no business complaining about long winters, but all the same, endless snow and bitter cold from November to February wore on her spirits more than a little. The benefits of living in this beautiful small village far outweighed the disadvantages, but it was sometimes hard to remember them when one was up to one's ears in snow and unable to poke a nose outside for fear it would freeze off.

Her goal was the Opera House, not for tickets

to see the next grand show to come their way, but to visit the town clerk's office on the first floor of the building. If anyone would be able to give Pauline information about the Warren family as well as Horace Van Camp, it was Susan Hao.

The petite Chinese-American woman looked up from her spotless desk and smiled welcomingly as Pauline entered her office.

"What can I do for you today?" Susan asked cheerfully.

Susan was about fifteen years older than Pauline, the granddaughter of immigrants who had originally settled in New York City's Chinatown but had chosen to exchange city life for the country when Susan's father was a small boy. Despite the age difference, the two women knew each other well from all the times Pauline came to the office looking up information for a story.

"What can you tell me about Horace Van Camp?" Pauline said.

Susan nodded. "The man who died recently? You'd do better asking about him in the Thousand Islands region, but I can at least tell you what everyone knows."

What "everyone knew," apparently, was that Mr. Van Camp was a former resident of New York City who had retired to live permanently at his summer house on the St. Lawrence River about ten years ago. What his business had been, no one was quite sure, but he was rumored to be fabulously wealthy, with a small but dazzling collection of rare art and jewelry.

He had been unmarried and had no children, and had died peacefully in his home of old age two weeks ago.

"I see," said Pauline.

"Are you doing his obituary for the *Watertown Daily Times*?" Susan asked.

"Not exactly," Pauline hedged.

It wasn't that she didn't trust Susan to be discreet, but she didn't feel comfortable sharing all of Arabella's story with any outsider just yet. It would make getting the information she needed that much trickier, but Pauline believed firmly in the right of every person to privacy.

It was, perhaps, an odd stance for a journalist to take, but Pauline could no more abandon it than she could her love of finding reasonable answers to difficult problems.

"Was he connected to anyone here in Canton or the general region, do you know?" she asked instead. "What led him to the Thousand Islands?"

Susan waved a slim hand. "Oh, plenty of rich people have summer homes along the river. It was especially popular thirty or forty years ago. The wealthy from New York City, Chicago, Pittsburgh, and elsewhere all liked to come play at a 'rustic' lifestyle. Not so much now, of course, with the economy the way it is."

Pauline's grandparents had had a summer cabin in the Adirondack mountains. She had loved visiting there when she was a little girl, and it had contributed to her desire to attend college and then live in this area. She had never been to the Thousand Islands, though, and hadn't realized it held the same appeal.

"I never heard of Mr. Van Camp having any particular connection with anyone in this area," Susan continued. She paused a moment, then said, "If you're wondering why he would leave Arabella Warren a diamond necklace, I can't help you. It's a mystery to me as much as anyone." Her deep brown eyes twinkled with amusement.

Pauline smiled wryly, acknowledging the point. Try keeping a secret in a small town! It was the price one paid for the close-knit community.

It was a wonder that no one had yet discovered Pauline's identity as the author of the popular Emma Daring novels. She could only put it down to the fact that she was not yet considered entirely "of" the town. A welcome outsider, but an outsider nonetheless. She hoped that by the time she'd lived here fifty years, she would be considered a proper local, but she had her doubts.

She also hoped that by the time fifty years had passed, she would be finished with journalism and Emma's adventures alike and have moved on to the scholarly work that was her true passion. She sometimes had her doubts about that, as well.

"Miss Warren asked me to look into the matter," she told Susan, now that secrecy was no longer necessary.

"The lawyer asked at the post office for her address while I was there buying stamps this morning," Susan said. "He said she'd been left a legacy."

Pauline was horrified at this garrulousness. Her

grandfather would never have approved. "He announced in public what the legacy was? How shockingly inappropriate!"

"Oh no," Susan assured her. "He only said a legacy. May Oates was in the post office at the same time, so she went right to her sister Minnie's house, next door to Arabella's. They kept watch out Minnie's kitchen window, and as soon as the lawyer left May went over to ask Arabella what had been left her, and Arabella was so shocked she told her. May told Minnie, who told Lucy Westin when they were both out doing their marketing, who told—"

"The entire town," Pauline said. "And what is the town's opinion?"

"Oh, that there is some scandal behind it, naturally, especially as soon as we heard Arabella went to see Ruby Richardson and then on to visit you. Where would be the excitement in something tame and ordinary?"

"Where, indeed," Pauline murmured. "Susan, what can you tell me about the Warren family? I am trying to find out if there's something in Miss Warren's parents' past that connects them to Mr. Van Camp."

"The Warrens have lived in Canton for ages," Susan said. "Long before my grandparents moved here, the Warren dairy farm was a byword. Arabella was her parents' only child, and when her father died one of her uncles took over the farm. Arabella moved to a small house in town, apparently quite happily. I can't think of anything that would connect the family to Mr. Van Camp, unless it had something to do with cows."

Without knowing what Mr. Van Camp's business had been, there was no way to be certain. Still, it didn't seem likely that he would leave Miss Warren something so valuable if he had only been a business associate—and surely her parents would have told her about him.

Unless they considered business matters above a woman's ability to understand. The leaving of the farm to an uncle indicated as much—but there, Pauline was speculating ahead of her facts. For all she knew, Miss Warren had asked her uncle to take over the farm. It was just as likely that she didn't care for farming as it was that her parents despised a woman's brain.

Pauline had to be careful to not always assume the worst of people.

"I'm glad he left her the necklace, whatever the reason," Susan said now. "I think it's high time something good came Arabella's way. She doesn't complain ever, but I think she's lonely. She was always scatter-brained when we were children, but it's gotten worse since her parents' death. Maybe the necklace will give her a new interest in life. If nothing else, I'm glad you're helping her. She needs people to care."

Pauline was humbled by Susan's words, and left the office vowing to do her best, both in solving the puzzle and in supporting Arabella Warren. She wasn't particularly good with people—she much preferred books and facts—but she would do what she could.

A quick stop by the Richardson house was next on her agenda. She hadn't seen Ruby since she and James returned from their honeymoon a month ago. Pauline looked over at the wide front porch, where Ruby was shaking out a carpet. Marriage suited her friend: she carried herself straighter, head higher, had rosy color in her cheeks, and a sparkle in her eyes that hadn't been there since her first husband died.

"Pauline! Lovely to see you," Ruby called, giving the carpet one final shake. "Do come in."

Seated at the kitchen table with a cup of coffee in her hands before she could blink, Pauline had a sudden insight into the trust Miss Warren had shown her by coming into the kitchen that morning. Guests sat in the living room. Friends sat around the kitchen table.

She had to swallow against the unexpected tightness in her throat.

"I thought I might see you today, after sending Miss Warren your way. I hope I didn't presume by referring her to you?" Ruby looked momentarily anxious.

"Not at all," Pauline assured her. "I am happy to take on the puzzle for her. I think it will prove a satisfactory challenge."

Ruby settled back with the smile returned to her face. "Good."

Pauline asked her friend the same questions about the Warren family she had asked Susan, and received much the same reply.

"The height of respectability, the Warrens. And

kind-hearted people, every one of them. You never heard a harsh word from any of their mouths, not to each other nor to anyone else. Mrs. Warren was always the first to help her neighbors if they were in trouble, and Mr. Warren used to hire tramps no one else would give the time of day to, in order to give them a helping hand. They were good people, and their daughter is the same."

"So perhaps the necklace really is a recognition of a kind deed done once to Mr. Van Camp," Pauline mused.

"Maybe, but ... I can't see Miss Warren not knowing about such a deed if that's the case. They were a close-knit family."

Unless they hadn't known who it was they were doing the good deed for. Wealthy men were often eccentric. What if Mr. Van Camp had been hiking cross-country and they took him for a tramp, and he never bothered to correct them? What if he'd waited all the years afterward to repay their kindness?

It was far-fetched, but more likely than the other scenarios Pauline's imagination had concocted.

"Hopefully the lawyer will have more information tomorrow," she said.

CHAPTER THREE

In the Lawyer's Office

It was about a two-hour drive from Canton to Clayton by automobile; the train would have been more comfortable but taken longer. On a winter's day with nothing else to do, Pauline would quite enjoy a leisurely train ride and a chance to work out her latest plot. Today, with a specific task and a reason to reach the end destination, she was thankful Miss Warren owned her own automobile. With the sharp wind blowing that morning, Pauline was even more thankful for the closed top and—luxury indeed —electric heater.

Miss Warren was a good driver, able to concentrate on the road as well as maintain a seemingly endless stream of chatter. Thankfully she required little in response, leaving Pauline free to pursue her own thoughts while she watched the muddy fields eventually turn to river slipping by.

Even aside from Ruby's glowing endorsement of the family, Pauline had a difficult time connecting Miss Warren with scandal. She seemed not only the epitome of respectability, but she practically radiated goodness, as well. If there was scandal connected to the legacy, Pauline was certain it did not personally involve Miss Warren. A distant relative, perhaps, but not the lady herself.

People's appearances were no true indicator of their character—more words of wisdom from her lawyer grandfather before his death—but even so, she couldn't shake the conviction that Miss Warren was as upright and moral as she seemed, and as Ruby had claimed.

Pauline could sense some of the loneliness Ruby had spoken of as well. It was in the woman's garrulous nature, as though she was starved for conversation. It was also in a certain wistful quality to her smile, an indefinable something in her demeanor. Whatever it was, Pauline couldn't help but pity her, diamond necklace inheritance or not.

Gradually the river on one side and trees on the other gave way to houses and other buildings as they passed through Alexandria Bay and then came into Clayton. Pauline scarcely had time to admire the smart white houses with their air of brisk prosperity and green lawns running down to the water's edge before Miss Warren turned a corner and they were downtown, with brick and cobblestone buildings rising on either side.

"Here we are!" Miss Warren said, pulling expertly into a parking space between a delivery van and horse-drawn wagon on Riverside Drive. A long row of offices sat parallel to the river: the one closest to the automobile discreetly displayed a sign reading "Law Offices of Ramsey and Ramsey" above its front door.

Pauline exited the vehicle thankfully. Two hours of endless chatter combined with the stuffiness from the heater had left her with the start of a headache. The fresh river air permeating the village did much to brighten her spirits and lessen the throbbing at her temples. She was thankful; often headaches were the precursor to worse difficulties.

In her younger days, Pauline had been particularly prone to what her mother referred to as "melancholia," and her father called "female vapors." Pauline didn't think either of those two descriptions were entirely fair, but there was no arguing with one's parents.

It had always felt to Pauline more as though her body and mind were under attack at such times. Sometimes caused by uncomfortable situations, sometimes for no reason at all, she would find herself in the grip of a fierce headache, followed by stomach cramps, shortness of breath, nausea, and trembling hands. The only cure she'd ever found for such attacks was to quietly rest in a dark room.

Thankfully, her move away from the noise and bustle of Albany, first to the restful campus of St. Lawrence University, where academics had given her life a new sense of order and purpose, and then to the apartment in the village of Canton after her graduation, had helped decrease her affliction significantly.

The moods, or attacks, or whatever they were,

still came on occasion, but far less frequently, and when they did come, she was finding better ways to combat them.

She would not have welcomed having to deal with one in a lawyer's office, however, so she was relieved to have her headache disperse in the bitingly cold March air.

Gulls wheeled overhead, crying out in their raucous voices. Skiffs, canoes, and other boats Pauline could not identify bobbed in the water just off the docks, their owners ready to say goodbye to winter's ice punts. The streets were scrupulously tidy, the shops all scrubbed free of winter's grime; she even saw one or two enterprising business owners preparing to give their clapboard fronts a fresh coat of paint to welcome the spring. Overall there was an air of energy and good cheer pervading the little town of Clayton, giving it a wide-awake and hearty feel.

Mr. Ramsey's office was spruce and welcoming, as well. Its cheerful yellow exterior harmonized nicely with the white, green, and blue colors of the other buildings along the row. Inside it was an almost blinding white, and scrupulously neat.

The secretary, a woman who managed to so wholly efface herself as to be almost invisible, greeted them in low, well-bred tones and murmured that Mr. Ramsey would see them in a few minutes.

Arabella Warren fell unusually silent the moment they walked through the door. She perched on one of the uncomfortable chairs waiting rooms always seemed to have, biting her lower lip and twisting her gloves in her hands. It did not take any spectacular act of deduction to gather that this odd business with the necklace was deeply troubling.

Pauline wished she could comfort her, but the colorless receptionist, for all her discretion, made it oddly impossible to speak freely. Her non-presence acted as a smothering blanket. Pauline would have preferred someone with more personality—she might have been able to speak then.

It was with great relief she saw the inner door open. Mr. Ramsey himself came through to greet them, dismissing a younger man Pauline presumed to be his clerk as he did.

"Hello and welcome, welcome!" he cried, tripping over his own feet as he approached them. He ignored this, shaking hands with each lady with every appearance of glee.

His receptionist's suffocating presence had no effect on *him*, apparently. "Miss Warren, so glad you could come today. And you brought a friend, how nice. A friend, surely? Not a sister—it would be too unfair for the gods to put two such beauties in one family."

Pauline felt instantly tired, and her headache returned. How she loathed this kind of raillery. Old Judge Gray, her grandfather, had been the solemn, quietly reassuring type of lawgiver. Pauline far preferred that to the unctuous inanities offered by Mr. Ramsey.

"Miss Gray," Miss Warren introduced her without any more explanation, for which Pauline was thankful.

She didn't want to tip her hand too soon. If Mr. Ramsey thought she was a reporter after a story, she'd never get any information out of him.

He shook their hands a second time and stood back to allow them to precede him into the inner office.

"George, you may take your lunch break now," he told the clerk. "Eleanor—" to the secretary— "see to it no one disturbs us."

In the office, thankfully, the painful white of the walls in the reception area was replaced by a softer beige, the uncomfortable seats by old leather chairs, and the overall air of an antiseptic operating theater by the smell of pipe tobacco and old books. It was almost too dim to see anything, aside from the reading lamp on the clerk's desk, but that only added to the mellow atmosphere.

The throbbing in Pauline's head receded once again in this familiar setting, and the tension lines in Miss Warren's face smoothed themselves out.

Mr. Ramsey stumbled on his way to his seat, caught himself, and settled in behind the broad oak desk, flushing a little as he did.

"Ah, excuse me. Terribly clumsy these days. That is—yes. So. Here for your inheritance, Miss Warren? Excellent, excellent. Mr. Van Camp, God rest his soul, would be so pleased to see it going into your worthy hands."

"Before I accept it, Mr. Ramsey ..." Miss Warren began. "Oh dear, this is difficult. I just want to know why, you see. It's all so confusing, and I'm afraid I don't feel entirely comfortable taking the necklace until I understand. It is such a valuable gift, isn't it, and it wouldn't be right to accept it if there was some mistake."

"Mistake?" Mr. Ramsey said, bewilderment crossing his broad, genial face.

Pauline deemed it time to step in. "What Miss Warren means, sir, is that she would like to know why Mr. Van Camp left her such a generous bequest."

"You mean you don't know?"

Miss Warren shook her head. "That's what I want you to tell me," she said, quite simply for her.

"But, my dear lady, I'm afraid I haven't the foggiest notion."

"You don't?" the two ladies said in unison.

Mr. Ramsey shook his head. "Not in the slightest."

This was a twist.

"You see," Mr. Ramsey went on, "I had never met Mr. Van Camp until a few months ago, when he rang me up and asked me to come to his house. I took my clerk and we made out the will according to the list he handed us with his bequests and legacies. No explanation was given of any of them."

"How many people?" Pauline interrupted. If the lawyer was going to be indiscreet, she would take advantage of it.

"Oh, a dozen, Miss Gray! A full dozen! Aside from the usual dispersion of house and moneys to various people and charities, there were a dozen personal bequests. Jewelry to eleven of them, as with Miss Warren here, and Mr. Van Camp's three Moillon paintings—surely you've heard of her? The Baroque painter woman?—to the twelfth. That's how Mr. Van Camp wanted it, so that's how George and I wrote it. And you really don't know why he chose you, Miss Warren? Remarkable, remarkable."

"No, and I—" Miss Warren began, when there was an interruption.

Even in the quiet closeness of the inner office Pauline heard the front door crash open and the receptionist raise her voice for once. The words were unintelligible, but the purport was made clear a moment later when the door to Mr. Ramsey's sanctum was flung open.

"I told you, you can't go in there, he's in a meeting!" the receptionist insisted.

"I don't care if he's with the President of the United States!" roared back the interloper over his shoulder.

He turned and faced the three startled individuals squarely.

"I ought to apologize for interrupting you, but I'm afraid I'm not particularly sorry," he said abruptly. He was quite a young man, a boy really, no older than seventeen, dressed in clothes that were clean but well-worn. He carried himself with the assurance of an older man, but the softness in his cheeks and jaw gave away his youth.

"I am Jonathan Van Camp, and I understand you are the lawyer responsible for giving my great-uncle's property to strangers?"

Arabella Warren gasped audibly. The young Van Camp glanced in her direction briefly before turning his attention back to the unfortunate Mr. Ramsey, who began to bluster.

"Now look here, young fellow, I am in the midst of a private meeting with these ladies, and you have no business coming in here and making these sorts of accusations! I ought to have you arrested for slander. I most certainly did not 'give away' your uncle's property. I made out his will according to his specifications, and I am one of his executors, but I bear no responsibility for the contents of it. Now then!"

Jonathan Van Camp stood his ground. "Uncle Horace told me over and over since we met that he was going to leave his baubles—the jewelry and paintings—to me, along with a trust to replace my allowance. Now he's dead and I'm cut out of the will entirely, why?"

"You had better ask yourself that," Mr. Ramsey said. "Perhaps your great-uncle thought your manners left something to be desired."

Pauline rose to her feet. Her detective instincts tingled. "Perhaps young Mr. Van Camp would be willing to go for a walk with me while you and Miss Warren conclude your business here," she said.

"Why would I do that?" the boy asked rudely.

Pauline faced him. She hadn't wanted to announce herself in this manner, but she saw no other choice. "Because Miss Warren has requested I investigate this business of the will."

While Jonathan Van Camp hesitated, Mr. Ramsey turned as red as a turkey's wattle, his eyes taking on a glassy sheen.

"A private detective? A lady detective! Now look here, this is highly inappropriate. Miss Warren, I can assure you that everything is aboveboard and perfectly legal here. You have no right bringing a detective—much less a *lady* detective—into the matter."

Pauline's respect for Miss Warren went up a notch as that lady came to her feet as well. "Mr. Ramsey, you have no business speaking so. You yourself admitted you know nothing about why the bequests were made the way they were, and if I want to be certain I am not cheating some poor soul out of his proper inheritance—morally, if not legally—that is my affair."

Pauline hadn't thought it possible for her to speak so clearly and coherently. It had an impressive effect on Mr. Ramsey as well as Jonathan Van Camp. The young man's face eased and something approaching a smile softened his mouth.

"I—you—most improper—no respect—most irregular—I have always conducted—that is—no one has ever accused—" the older man sputtered.

"I would be happy to take a walk with you," Jonathan now told Pauline. "I think a detective, especially a lady detective, is exactly what is needed in this case."

CHAPTER FOUR

Jonathan

"Now," Pauline said once they were on the street. "Let me take a look at you."

He was tall and lanky, with the over-large hands and feet of adolescence. His blue eyes were cold and shadowed and there were faint lines of bitterness around his mouth, but Pauline thought she could see the seeds of a good-hearted man inside the angry boy.

"You and your great-uncle were close?" she said.

He shrugged, withdrawn and silent now the fire of his anger had burned out.

"Where are your parents?" Pauline tried.

"Gone," he muttered.

"Do you truly suspect Mr. Ramsey of attempting to cheat you out of your inheritance?" she persisted.

Another shrug.

Pauline threw her hands into the air. "How am I supposed to help you if you won't even talk to me?

Goodness knows you were voluble enough in the lawyer's office. I thought you *wanted* a detective involved in this business."

"I do, but ..." he trailed off.

Pauline didn't have much experience with boys. Her male cousins were all older than she was, and her few childhood friends had all been girls. She had made friends with both sexes in college, but Jonathan Van Camp was a bit younger than they all had been.

One thing that did seem to be a universal with boys and men alike was their appetite. The hotel dining rooms were out of the question, with Jonathan's shabby clothes. An ice cream soda at Ellis's drugstore would be the obvious choice, but it was hardly conducive to private conversation.

The establishment down the road from where Arabella had parked might be just the thing.

"Let's get a cup of coffee and a bite to eat," Pauline said, turning her steps toward the Hub Cafe (Ladies Lunchroom and Ice Cream Parlor Upstairs). "Perhaps we'll find some common ground for conversation then."

As with any growing boy, Jonathan's eyes brightened at the mention of food, and he regained a measure of zest as he walked beside her, courteously offering his arm to help her over any rough spots on the sidewalk and shortening his stride to match hers.

The pretty waitress with a pink bow in her hair that matched her rosy cheeks seated them at once at a corner table on the second floor, and brought them

coffee and a plate of muffins with admirable prompt-
ness. In between devouring muffins and the enor-
mous piece of apple pie the waitress brought after
seeing how quickly he moved through the muffins,
Jonathan finally unbent enough to tell Pauline his
story.

His father had been the only child of Horace
Van Camp's only brother.

"Dad died when I was a baby. Mother married
again a year or so later, and we moved to Pennsylva-
nia. She died about four years ago."

Pauline listened without comment as the story
continued, the tragedy made all the more stark by the
simple, straightforward way Jonathan told it.

"After Mother's funeral, my stepfather told me
I was old enough to get by on my own, that he had
enough to do to feed my half-sisters and himself."

Thirteen years old and on his own, Jonathan
managed to track down his father's people. He introduced himself to his great-uncle without knowing
how wealthy he was, but wouldn't take charity from
the man once he did learn of it.

"It was one thing to ask Dad's uncle for a place
to live and food to eat in exchange for work when I
thought maybe he was a farmer or something," he explained, wiping his mouth on a spotlessly clean napkin. "But not like that. It—it just didn't feel right."

Despite his inability to articulate his reasons,
Pauline understood, and admired him for them. This
boy had fine moral principles. Her mother, poor
choice in second husband aside, had clearly done well

by her son.

Horace Van Camp seemed to agree. He insisted on giving Jonathan a small allowance, helped him find a job and secure a room at the Bouchard guest house, and had him out for dinner every Sunday.

"He *said* he would provide for me in his will," Jonathan said. "He *promised*. He said an inheritance was different from charity, and he didn't want his collections to pass out of Van Camp hands. He'd promised the house to a hospital, and was going to put most of the money toward charitable organizations, but family was important, he said. The jewelry and the paintings should stay with kin, because they were personal. He didn't want them divided among strangers. He specifically said so."

Jonathan had been doing some carpentry work on a farm outside town for the past couple of weeks, and had returned to his landlady's information that his great-uncle was dead and the will had already been read. The house and grounds had been given to a hospital, as the old man had wanted; the money donated to local charities likewise. Against his stated purpose, however, nothing had been left to Jonathan, and the jewels and paintings were split between twelve individuals.

"If he'd been angry with me or if I'd done something to offend him, he would have told me, he wouldn't have changed his will secretly," Jonathan said, picking at the crumbs left on his plate. "He didn't brood, he blew up and then calmed down."

Like his great-nephew, apparently.

"Do you really think Mr. Ramsey is responsible?" Pauline asked.

Jonathan rubbed his fingers together, avoiding her eye as he looked around the small cafe.

"No," he finally admitted. "I suppose not. It's not like the will was changed to benefit him, and I don't know why anyone would do something like that. I was just ... angry."

"The problem at hand is," Pauline said, thinking it through, "why did Mr. Van Camp change his mind right before his death to cut his only relative out of his will and instead leave his most beloved possessions to strangers? Once we find the answer to that, we will hopefully know why he chose those twelve people, and Arabella's conscience will be at rest, and you will have peace of mind. It is quite the puzzle, I must say."

On the surface, the easiest answer seemed to be that while Jonathan was out of town, Mr. Van Camp had learned something to the boy's discredit and in a blind rage made up a new will to ensure he didn't receive anything.

But what could that be? Could Jonathan Van Camp be a fraud? What if he wasn't really the old man's great-nephew?

That didn't make sense—surely someone as canny in business as Horace Van Camp would have thoroughly inspected the boy's credentials when he first arrived. And it was an awfully long time for a con artist to wait for a payoff, four years which could have stretched on even longer, had Mr. Van Camp's health permitted.

Plus, that still didn't answer the question of why Arabella and the other eleven had been chosen instead of Jonathan. If Mr. Van Camp didn't know them at all, how did he get their names? How did he learn of their existence? Why, in heaven's name, leave a diamond necklace to a perfect stranger?

No, the simplest answer didn't seem to be an answer at all. Well then, moving along.

What if Mr. Ramsey *had* altered the will? That was the next simplest idea. However, Jonathan was correct when he pointed out that the lawyer didn't benefit from this new will, and why should he want to cut Jonathan out in favor of strangers? It would have been more in his interest to ingratiate himself with the new heir.

So much for Mr. Ramsey as a villain. Who, then?

"Jonathan, did your uncle have any staff at the house?"

"A sort of butler-valet fellow and a gardener. Why?"

"Were they left anything?"

He shrugged, looking startled. "I don't know. That lawyer man would."

Pauline frowned. Now that Mr. Ramsey was annoyed with her involvement in this matter, he was much less likely to volunteer information.

"Do you think that's important?"

"If they were left out of the will as well, then your uncle wasn't angry at you," Pauline said, working her way through her thoughts as she spoke. "It would have been something else that made him alter it. If he left them in but cut you out …"

"Then it was spite." He slumped down in his chair. "Swell."

Pauline stood and gathered her handbag and gloves. "Do you know where to find them?"

"I suppose." Jonathan stood up as well, curious and wary but still a gentleman.

"If the lawyer won't tell us, perhaps they will. I'll leave a note on Miss Warren's auto so she won't think you've abducted me, and then we shall go find these two."

She chose not to hear his muttered comment about the abduction working the other way 'round.

Back out in the fresh air, Jonathan told Pauline that the gardener, Jasper Randolph, lived in a small cottage in Clayton. Mr. Gagne, the butler-valet, was still living at the Van Camp residence, a mile outside the village.

"At least, that's what my landlady says."

Pauline, mindful of the changeable March weather, decided they would visit the gardener first and let Miss Warren drive them to the estate when her business with the lawyer was concluded.

Jasper Randolph's house was neat and tidy, a small white clapboard cottage a short distance from the river, with an immaculately tended garden both in front and in back. Nothing was growing yet, of course, not even the crocuses, but Pauline could see where he had been stirring the dirt and starting his pruning. She would have thought it early even for that, but perhaps it was warmer here by the mighty St. Lawrence than in Canton.

Mr. Randolph's house, unfortunately, was locked up tight, with a sign on the front door saying, "No Milk Until Further Notice."

"Not simply gone for the day, then," Pauline said, turning away from the closed door.

"Now what?" Jonathan said, shoulders slumping.

If there was one thing Pauline had learned from her profession, it was perseverance. She led Jonathan to the house next door and knocked.

The door was opened by a pleasant-faced older woman with snow-white hair, dark skin, and shaky hands. "May I help you?" she said in a soft voice with a distinct southern accent.

"We are looking for Mr. Randolph," Pauline said. "Can you tell us when he'll return?"

"Oh, not for a long time, miss, I'm sorry to have to tell you. He's gone off to New Mexico."

"New Mexico!" Pauline said.

The woman nodded, a smile creasing her cheeks. "Oh, it was so exciting. Jasper, he was so saddened by poor Mr. Van Camp, his employer, dying, and he didn't know if he'd be able to get another job. He's a fine gardener, Jasper is, but he's almost as old as me—we were children together down in Virginia, him and me and my husband, and we all came north together and settled down here, and here Jasper and I still are, even though my husband's gone now. But not everyone is willing to hire someone Jasper's age, don't you see, so he was worried."

"Mm," Pauline said encouragingly, while at her elbow Jonathan stifled a yawn and couldn't keep his eyes from wandering toward the river.

"Then, two days ago, he knocked on my door beaming. 'Emmy,' he said—that's my name, Emmy Tuttle—'Emmy, I'm off to New Mexico!' And I said, just as you did, miss, 'New Mexico!' He laughed and said that even though he hadn't been able to leave him anything in the will because he was one of the witnesses, Mr. Van Camp had arranged a reward for his faithful service after all by setting in motion a trip to New Mexico for him to take after he died."

It took Pauline a few moments to untangle Mrs. Tuttle's pronouns. "Mr. Van Camp couldn't leave Mr. Randolph anything in Mr. Van Camp's will because Mr. Randolph had been one of the witnesses to the will, so instead Mr. Van Camp arranged for a trip for Mr. Randolph after Mr. Van Camp died?"

"Yes, that's what I said, miss. That nice young man from the lawyer's office came out to tell him so, and wasn't Jasper tickled pink! 'That stuffy Mr. Gagne didn't get a holiday, for all he thought he was so much better than me,' he told me. 'Both witnesses, we were, and only I get the trip. They say virtue is its own reward, but it's nice to see something more solid!' That was just his way of speaking, you understand."

Pauline assured her she did.

"So, Jasper's going to be gone at least a month, but he said he might not come back at all if New Mexico is really as beautiful and warm as everyone says it is. We feel the cold in our bones these days, we do, but I love it here and wouldn't move back south if you paid me, even if I am sorry to see Jasper leave. This is where Mr. Tuttle is buried, and this is where I plan to be buried, right next to him—though not for a good many more years, the good Lord willing. I'm sorry I can't be more help, miss."

"You've been a considerable help," Pauline assured her. "Thank you so much, Mrs. Tuttle. Come along, Jonathan."

She mulled this new information as they walked back to the road.

"That was interesting," she said.

"Jasper left, what does it matter?" he returned, kicking a stone out of the road.

Pauline case a severe eye at him. "In a case like this, everything matters."

CHAPTER FIVE

At the Van Camp Estate

Arabella Warren was waiting for them by the auto, as was Mr. Ramsey. Beside Pauline, Jonathan sucked in an audible breath through his teeth. She didn't have time to inquire the reason before he extended his stride, outpacing her in seconds, and approached the lawyer with his head high and his fists clenched.

"I apologize for my behavior earlier, sir," he said, in a tone that stopped just short of imperious and did not indicate any sort of genuine sorrow. "I ought not to have made such accusations."

Mr. Ramsey smiled, then frowned. "Not at all, not at all! That is to say—it was terribly rude, young fellow, but there, I'm sure you were upset—not that I can excuse those sort of statements! Some people in my position would sue you for slander, not that I would go to such lengths, but all the same ... But there, we can let bygones be bygones, I am sure. After all, to expect an inheritance and receive nothing is a terrible blow, terrible. Dreadful how forgetful these old men can be. Why, George—that is, I—had to ask him once or twice to clarify something he had written in the draft of the will, and would you believe it, he couldn't even remember writing it in the first place! Well, there it is, and it is indeed hard lines on you, young man, so we'll let this little incident slide. In fact, if you are in need of financial assistance in any way, I'm sure I can—"

"No, thank you." Jonathan's voice was curt as he pulled his hand free from the lawyer's half-hearted shake.

Geniality fully restored now, Mr. Ramsey ignored this and turned to Pauline. "Miss Gray, I really do believe I owe you an apology myself. Miss Warren explained that you aren't really a private detective, merely a friend with—now, how did you put it, Miss Warren?—a good head for puzzles, that's right. Under the circumstances, I can understand how Miss Warren might want someone to help clarify the situation. It is a puzzle to be sure, but the answer is merely the peculiarities of older folk. All the same, I think I reacted a mite hastily back in the office."

Pauline favored him with a gracious, if cool, smile. "Not at all, sir."

Mr. Ramsey smiled fatuously. "Excellent, excellent. Should have known such a lovely young lady as yourself, with such an excellent taste in clothing, couldn't truly be a private detective. Such a pretty shade of yellow, your blouse—looks just like a daffodil."

Pauline was puzzled by this effusion—not only

were such personal comments inappropriate, her blouse was white.

She looked again at his beaming face and deduced that he considered the best way to restore relations with a female was to compliment her clothing, regardless of how inaccurate his statement.

Having settled that, she looked at Miss Warren, deliberately using formal language to move away from this false intimacy. "Has your business been transacted satisfactorily?"

Miss Warren opened her handbag and peeked in, then looked up with a flustered expression, closing it again hastily. "Yes," she said. "That is—yes. I think I'd best get right home and take this to the bank. I don't feel quite comfortable carrying it. Dear me, I don't wish to seem ungrateful, but I'm still so puzzled by it all. You say he was peculiar and forgetful, Mr. Ramsey, but I'm sure I don't see how either peculiarity or forgetfulness can make you leave something to a stranger. And I still don't know how he even learned my name! It seems downright spooky, if you ask me. Oh dear, but yes, Miss Gray, I am ready to leave."

"Excellent. Do you mind going back by way of the Van Camp estate? Jonathan would like to show us where his great-uncle lived."

"I would?" the young man began, when Pauline discreetly kicked his ankle. "Oh, that. I mean, yes, I would."

Pauline didn't care to let Mr. Ramsey know she was still investigating the matter, but nor was she inclined to let it go now. Arabella Warren was right: no amount of forgetfulness or peculiarity could incline someone to leave gifts to individuals he had never heard of.

Through the open office door, Pauline saw George-the-clerk (she couldn't remember his surname, if indeed Mr. Ramsey had bothered to introduce them at all) stand up from his desk. "Sir, Mr. Ramsey, do you recall that letter from the hospital?"

"Oh yes, oh yes," said Mr. Ramsey, fingers twitching. "I'm sorry, Miss Warren, Miss Gray, but we had a letter from the hospital, the one Mr. Van Camp left the estate to, asking that we be sure not to allow trespassers or sight-seers on the property. It is theirs now, you know, and we must respect their wishes."

Miss Warren frowned. "Surely they would not object to their benefactor's great-nephew taking one final look at the place. I hardly think he counts as general public."

"Alas, dear lady, the law is the law, and we must follow the letter of it rather than the spirit, however much we might wish otherwise. Besides, you must get that necklace to your bank right away! The longer it is in your personal possession, the more danger you are in."

"I must say I don't understand at all why one would want a diamond necklace if one is never to be allowed to wear it, but must always keep it in the bank," said Miss Warren with a frown. "But oh well, there seems to be far too much about all this that I don't understand, and nobody asked my opinion on any of it! If they had, I could have given them an earful, let me tell you."

"Exactly so, Miss Warren," said Pauline. "Good day, Mr. Ramsey. Come along, Jonathan."

Miss Warren had opened the driver's side door of the auto when Pauline remembered that they needed one more thing from the lawyer before they could leave.

"Oh, Miss Warren, you were going to ask Mr. Ramsey for a list of the other heirs, weren't you? So that you could see if any of you had anything in common that might have caused Mr. Van Camp to choose you all?"

Miss Warren blinked a few times before picking up her cue. "Yes—yes, of course. Would that be acceptable, Mr. Ramsey?"

"Naturally, my dear lady," Mr. Ramsey said. "George, jot down a list for Miss Warren."

"Sir, are you certain? You are always saying it isn't appropriate to divulge that sort of information."

"George, my boy, I admire your caution, but in this case, I think we can make an exception. After all, in an ordinary state of things, all the heirs would have gathered together to hear the will read, and would therefore each know what the others had inherited. In this case, I think it entirely appropriate to give Miss Warren a list, especially if it sets her mind at ease."

George pulled a sour face but did as he was bid, bringing out a handwritten list a few minutes later. He handed it to Mr. Ramsey, who didn't bother looking at it before passing it along to Miss Warren.

"I hope it sheds some light on the matter for

you, Miss Warren, so that your conscience may rest and you can fully enjoy your magnificent inheritance. Good day, Miss Gray, young man."

Miss Warren handed the list to Pauline "to take care of on the ride," and at last they were on their way.

"Thank you for the ride, Miss Warren, but I don't actually need it," Jonathan said once they had pulled away from the curb. "My boarding house is only over on Union Street."

"We are going to your great-uncle's estate, Jonathan." Pauline spoke with quiet firmness.

"Oh dear," said Miss Warren, one hand fluttering loose from the wheel. "But the lawyer said—"

"Even if the hospital does want strangers kept away from what is theirs, we are not visiting the property. We are visiting Mr. Van Camp's butler, who is still acting as caretaker."

"Oh." Miss Warren considered this. "I suppose that makes sense. But why do we want to speak with him?"

Pauline explained. "Despite Mr. Ramsey's anecdote, I doubt Mr. Van Camp was forgetful enough to accidentally leave his personal manservant out of his will. I want to see if he left Mr. Gagne anything. If Mr. Gagne was left out, I might believe Jonathan was simply forgotten. If not, there would seem to be a different answer to this riddle, one that still eludes us."

"Is his name on that list?" Miss Warren asked.

Pauline glanced down at it. "No, but that only means he did not inherit some of the jewelry or paintings. He still could have received a monetary legacy."

"But that Mrs. Tuttle said Jasper said Great-Uncle Horace couldn't leave either of them anything because they were both witnesses, and only Jasper got rewarded for it," Jonathan contributed from the back.

"True, but there must be more to the story than that," Pauline said. "Besides, a good journalist—or investigator—never believes third-hand information. We must always track it down to its source."

Miss Warren wanted to know who Jasper and Mrs. Tuttle were, and that explanation lasted the rest of the drive to the estate.

"I must say I don't care for any of this," Miss Warren said as she maneuvered the auto up the long, winding drive to the Van Camp residence. "I do wish —I know I should be thankful, but I do wish that Mr. Van Camp hadn't left me anything at all. I don't need a diamond necklace, and when am I ever going to wear one? Look here, young man—you said in the lawyer's office that your uncle promised to leave the jewelry and such to you. Why don't I just give you the necklace? That feels much more fair."

There was a startled sound from the back seat. Then, Jonathan spoke up slowly.

"That—that is awfully good of you, Miss Warren. But I don't think I can accept. If Great-Uncle Horace really did leave me out of the will on purpose, then it would feel like cheating for me to accept your necklace. Besides, you don't even know me!" His voice turned incredulous on that last point.

"I suppose you're right," Miss Warren said. "But

if we find there was a mistake, this necklace is yours whether you want it or not, young man."

Jonathan said nothing, perhaps too stunned by this generosity of spirit to reply. Pauline was touched as well. She couldn't think of many people who would respond so to this sort of situation. It made her even more determined to discover the truth behind the puzzle.

"Besides," Miss Warren continued, "It is far too grand for me, and for Canton. I mean really, Miss Gray, can you see me going to church or doing the marketing wearing diamonds?"

The image was so incongruous Pauline had to laugh. A gruff chuckle from the back seat indicated Jonathan was tickled by it as well. Miss Warren's cheeks flushed and her eyes showed her pleasure at having amused her companions so.

The drive crested a hill, and the Van Camp estate opened before their eyes. Miss Warren put on the brake. "Oh my," she said softly.

Pauline had to agree.

The house itself was unpretentious, if large, built of grey stone and standing solidly in the middle of a sprawling lawn. It was the vista behind it that drew one's eye and stole one's breath.

The greening land rolled away behind the hill the house was built on, fields and trees alike receding down to end at the magnificent St. Lawrence River. The silver waters, undulating swiftly past, were dotted with some of the thousand islands that gave the region its name. Far off on the distant horizon lay the misty borders of Canada.

Pauline could see why someone would want to retire to this place.

Jonathan scrambled out of the backseat first, opening the door for Miss Warren without thinking.

"I'm glad he gave this place to the hospital," he said abruptly, offering his hand to the older woman absently. "That, at least, is what he had promised, even if he forgot or changed his mind about everything else."

"You don't want to have all this," Pauline waved an encompassing hand, "for your own?"

"It would be too much for me," Jonathan said, scorn edging his tone. "Could you see me living here all on my own?" A reminiscent smile played around his finely-drawn mouth. "I asked Great-Uncle Horace that when he asked me the same question, and he just about killed himself laughing. We agreed the hospital was better. All I want is a small place, something no one can take from me. A little bit of land all my own, to call home." He closed his mouth with a snap.

"Let's see if Mr. Gagne is home to visitors, shall we?" Pauline said.

They pressed the doorbell and thumped the lion's-head knocker, but no response came to either.

"Oh well, he must be out," Miss Warren said.

Jonathan frowned. "But his auto is still here, look." He pointed to the small shed Pauline had overlooked earlier in her amazement at the view. The black nose of an automobile poked out from the front.

"He has his own auto?"

"Great-Uncle Horace hated them," Jonathan said, laughter crossing his face and making him look like the boy he was. "So Gagne bought his own and used it whenever they needed to drive anywhere, Great-Uncle moaning and complaining the entire time."

"Well then, perhaps he's gone for a walk," Miss Warren suggested. "I know I should, if I lived in this place, even as the hired help. I should walk all over it, every day, just to marvel at its beauty."

"Gagne isn't much for walking," said Jonathan, his tone doubtful.

"Let us spread out and see what we can discover," Pauline said. "Perhaps he needed to tend something on the grounds."

The gathering shadows cleared from Jonathan's face. "Sure."

The three scattered, Miss Warren going to the left of the house, Jonathan to the right, and Pauline straight behind. Her companions' voices echoed in her ears as they began calling for Mr. Gagne. She added her own voice to the mix as she entered the woods and outside noise became muffled.

"Mr. Gagne? Mr. Gagne, are you here?"

She kept to the path that wove its way through the trees, until a splash of color to her left caught her eye. She turned, trying to make it out in the green gloom. There, a bit of red on the ground near that fallen log...

Pauline stepped off the path to inspect it more

closely. It was probably nothing but a maple leaf left over from autumn, but her curiosity was piqued. Most fallen leaves had faded and turned into ground cover after the winter.

She was nearly on top of him before her brain caught up with what her eyes were seeing.

It was no fallen log at all, and no maple leaf.

The body of a man lay prone upon the ground, blood from a head wound staining the earth.

Pauline swallowed something between a gasp and a scream. She forced herself to step close enough to bend down and check his wrist for a pulse.

The coldness of his skin sent chills down her own spine. There was no pulse, and as she looked more closely she saw that the blood on and around his head had dried. The red, which she had initially taken for fresh blood, was in fact a handkerchief left carelessly beside the fallen man.

It seemed she had found Mr. Gagne, but he would never answer her questions now.

CHAPTER SIX

Suspects and Theories

"Well, you have been making a day of it. On the trail of a new story?"

The question died on Sarah's lips as she took in Pauline's state as the other entered the apartment. "What on earth is the matter?"

Pauline glanced at herself in the mirror over the mantelpiece. Pale at all times, her skin was practically translucent now, and the shadows under her hazel eyes made it appear she hadn't slept in a week.

In short, she looked ghastly.

"I found a dead body in Alexandria Bay," she said, wearily dropping onto her favorite seat on the hearthrug before the cozy fire.

"What, another?" was Sarah's response, more exasperated than sympathetic.

"I didn't 'find' the last one, and the police have declared this one an accident," Pauline said, irritation bringing some of her usual crispness back to her voice.

Sarah, a nurse to her core, said, "Let me bring

you a tray for your supper, and then you can tell me the entire story. Something hints that you don't necessarily agree with the police's opinion."

Under Sarah's professional eye, Pauline had a plate of beef stroganoff, a slice of bread, and a glass of milk right there in front of the fire, and found herself revived enough to tell her friend about the day.

Sarah took up her sewing, most likely transforming a simple frock into something stunning and glamorous, as usual, while she listened.

As Pauline finished her story, Sarah shook her head.

"I don't like any of it. Too convenient: the gardener gone and the butler dead? The lawyer must be behind it. Daddy always said to never trust a lawyer."

"But there's no motive," Pauline protested, arguing against her own suspicions as much as Sarah's. "Even Jonathan admits that. The lawyer doesn't get anything from the will, any more than Jonathan himself. So why would he forge a will and remove the witnesses—Jasper Randolph at considerable expense to himself, no less—if he didn't even benefit from it?"

"What other options are there?" Sarah persisted.

Pauline wiped her hands on a napkin and set the tray aside to tick the possibilities off on her fingers. "One: the police are right and Mr. Gagne's death was an accident, and Horace Van Camp decided for reasons unknown to disinherit his great-nephew and select twelve persons to receive his collections instead, despite previous insistence that they should remain with family."

Sarah's snort showed how unlikely she thought that option.

"Two: Jonathan Van Camp was so angry at his great-uncle that he went to the estate in a rage before coming to the lawyer's office, got into a fight with the butler, and killed him."

Sarah interrupted indignantly. "What a horrible suspicion to have of that poor boy!"

"That's what the police initially suspected before they settled on an accident," Pauline said. "I don't like it, but we have to consider it."

"Did he try to prevent you from visiting the estate at all?"

"No."

Sarah stabbed the needle triumphantly into the next stitch. "There you have it. Surely if he had killed the man, he wouldn't have wanted all of you going there and wandering around to find the body."

It was an excellent point, one Pauline hadn't yet considered. She was thankful to Sarah for bringing it up. "The third option is a mysterious person who persuaded Mr. Van Camp to change the will, and then got Mr. Randolph out of the country and killed Mr. Gagne to keep them from telling anyone about it."

"About what? Do be more specific."

Pauline shrugged. "That's part of the mystery. The way the will was changed? The reason for it? Our mysterious individual—Mr. or Miss X, let's say, though it sounds ridiculously melodramatic—must have been there in person when Mr. Van Camp changed the will, and he or she doesn't want anyone to know."

Sarah considered this, mulling over all the options over before nodding decisively. "As much as I still want to blame the lawyer, your mysterious Mr. X does seem most likely. One of the twelve persons inheriting under the new will?"

"That was my thought," Pauline said. "And the other eleven are a blind."

"But goodness! What could one bequest be worth that this person would be willing to give away the rest?"

"If we could determine that, we would be one step closer to discovering Mr. X," Pauline said.

"Are we leaving Arabella Warren off the suspect list?"

"I think we must," Pauline said. "Not only do I doubt she has the character to plot, scheme, and murder, I do not see why she would bring me in on the matter if she had a hand in it. Perhaps she is a cunning actress and has a deeper purpose than we can divine —"

"But it's not likely," Sarah finished. "I agree. So what is our next step?"

"I thought you disapproved of me getting mixed up in this affair?" Pauline asked.

Sarah folded her strong brown hands together over her knee, letting her sewing slip. "I disapprove of you wandering in here looking like the ghost of yourself. However," her black eyes flashed, "I disapprove even more of murder and robbery, especially of those too poor or innocent to help themselves."

Pauline reflected, not for the first time, how lucky she had been the day she answered Sarah's newspaper ad for a roommate. Some in this small, rural village might raise eyebrows at their situation: two working women, one black and one white, both defying convention in their career choices—Sarah as a hospital nurse in a mostly-white community; Pauline as a newspaper columnist—but their friendship enriched both their lives.

Pauline knew someday Sarah would marry and move to a home of her own; the other girl was not as content in her singleness as Pauline was.

Until that day came, Pauline would continue to be thankful.

She pulled out the list the reluctant George had given Miss Warren earlier. "Miss Warren didn't recognize any of these names, so I think the next step is to contact each of them to learn if they knew Mr. Van Camp or each other, or if they have anything in common. I hope there will be something about one of them that will shed some light on whether he or she is our mysterious X."

"Surely we can eliminate some of them even before that point," Sarah said. "What is included on the list?"

Pauline handed the piece of creamy stationery over to her. "Names, ages, addresses."

"Arden Jamison, age eighty-seven, Adams, NY," Sarah read out. She stopped and raised her eyebrows. "Eighty-seven? I believe we can cross him off. One cannot imagine an octogenarian plotting murder for gain, never mind having the strength to murder a younger man."

Pauline acknowledged the point with a wave of her hand. "Oh," she said, stopping her wave halfway through. "I think I've heard of him. Yes, that's right. He dug up an ancient helmet they think might be Roman in his backyard, and the anthropologists are wild about it. I remember because the *Jefferson County Journal* scooped us on it, and our editors were furious."

"A Roman helmet in New York State? Surely not," Sarah said, diverted from the main point.

"Hence why anthropologists are wild about it," Pauline said.

Sarah shook her head. She picked up a pencil and drew a line through Arden Jamison's name. "Maria Thompson, five, Sacketts Harbor. Five?"

"Very well, cross out Maria Thompson—though I suppose her parents could be responsible."

"Honestly, Pauline. That is far-fetched even for one of your novels."

Sarah was the only person outside of Pauline's publishers who knew of her novels. A secret of that sort was difficult to keep from the person with whom one lived. Luckily for Pauline, Sarah was utterly trustworthy.

"Maria is off the list, then," Pauline agreed.

Richard Bracken and Caroline Swanson were also taken off the list due to old age, leaving them with Jane Casper, thirty-three, Cape Vincent; Denis

O'Leary, forty, Watertown; Alan Caruthers, twenty-one, Carthage; Bertha Nelson, fifty-nine, Potsdam; Brian Nettleton, nineteen, Clayton; David Anderson, twenty-nine, Alexandria Bay; and Miller Horton, thirty-one, Toronto.

"Good grief," Sarah said. "Where on earth did Mr. Van Camp or Mr. X pick up on such a disparate group?"

"I have a feeling if we could answer that question, we'd have our finger on the entire problem," Pauline said.

"How will we begin to approach them?"

"Oh, that's simple enough. We tell them we are running a story in the *Times* on the unusual legacies of Mr. Van Camp. My editor might even approve the story, who knows? Shall we split the list?"

"We can't possibly interview them all even if we split the list," Sarah said. "Unless you are planning a trip to Toronto?"

"Some will have to be done via letter or telephone," Pauline said. "But we can do some of them here."

"I can stop by and query the one in Potsdam tomorrow after my shift at the hospital ends. I'll already be halfway there," Sarah said. The Canton-Potsdam Hospital, where she worked, was located squarely between the two towns.

"I want to check in on Jonathan anyway, so I can interview Miss Casper, Mr. Nettleton, and Mr. Anderson," Pauline said, running her finger down the list.

"That leaves Denis O'Leary, Alan Caruthers, and

Miller Horton," Sarah said, taking the list from Pauline to look at it herself. "I will write to the first two, and you can write to Mr. Horton."

"Excellent," Pauline said. "Thank you."

Sarah set the list on the side table and began to sew again. Her dark eyes were troubled. "You say you will try to write the story we are using as an excuse?"

Pauline understood her difficulty. It seemed wrong to use half-lies and outright deceptions in order to reach truth. It was something she had wrestled with in her conscience even when she told the lawyer that they wished to pay their respects to Mr. Gagne when they really went to gain a greater understanding of Mr. Van Camp's will, or letting Mr. Ramsey initially believe she was Miss Warren's friend rather than that she was accompanying her to seek out the reasons behind her bequest.

Was it ever right to use deception in order to provoke honesty? Logic said yes, but her heart said no.

"I will do my best," was all she could promise to Sarah.

Her friend nodded. "And—you don't feel this is —at all—meddling? Is it really our place to go about hunting down a murderer? I realize we can't leave it to the police when they are convinced the death was accidental, but it still feels—over-officious, I suppose."

Here, Pauline was on surer ground. She had spent considerable time pondering this matter after her previous case. "So long as we aren't meddling purely for our own enjoyment, say out of a desire to manipulate people, I have no qualms. If we have the ability and the inclination to bring about justice for those who can't receive it any other way, it cannot be wrong to act." Honesty compelled her to add, "I do, admittedly, get a great deal of satisfaction out of unraveling a puzzle, but that isn't my only motivation."

Sarah laughed, set aside her sewing for good, and pulled the writing materials out of their drawer in Pauline's desk. "There's no rule that says you can't enjoy yourself even while doing something good for others. If I didn't get satisfaction out of nursing, I wouldn't have been able to make it my career, no matter how many people I was able to help."

On that note, they set to writing their letters, comparing them for clarity, addressing them, and setting them aside to give to the postman in the morning. That finished, Pauline took her turn at washing the dishes, as Sarah had prepared dinner, while Sarah finished her sewing.

An ordinary evening, the perfect antidote to the troubling events that had marred the day. Pauline even dared hope she would be able to sleep without being plagued by nightmares of finding Mr. Gagne's body.

She did: her sleep was deep and untroubled and she woke the next morning ready to face anything. Sarah had breakfasted and left already for her shift, leaving behind a note saying she wouldn't forget to look up Bertha Nelson after work.

Pauline scraped what was left of the oatmeal

Sarah had prepared into a bowl, adding cream and maple syrup to make it more palatable to her taste buds, and sliced an apple to accompany it. She looked longingly at the coffee can, but after hearing the grounds rattle inside when she shook it, she sighed and pulled down the jar of chicory instead. She far preferred the real thing, but at least chicory was a reasonable substitute, and far better for the pocketbook.

She generally enjoyed reading the newspaper with her morning coffee, a habit picked up from summers spent with her grandparents when she was a girl. Her grandfather had taken several papers, and would read excerpts aloud to Pauline and her grandmother in between sips of his coffee.

This morning's paper delivery was late—the *Watertown Daily Times* had a new paperboy, and efficiency was not his watchword—so Pauline picked through the pile of read papers by the fireplace to find something else, finally settling on an old copy of the *North Country Advance* that she had somehow missed when it first came out. Even old news was better than nothing.

A picture of a stunning patchwork quilt caught her eye first; quilting being one of the many skills she admired without being able to master. The accompanying story told of how the quilt's creator, a Mrs. Bertha Nelson, had sold the magnificent work to the governor of New York after he had seen it displayed at the State Fair last summer.

Bertha Nelson ... that was one of the people on

the list from the lawyer's office. Pauline was musing on the nature of coincidences when she was interrupted by a knock on the door.

9:00 in the morning was early for visitors, with most people either at their jobs or getting housework done and out of the way for the day. Pauline put the paper down, set her dishes in the sink, and answered the knock.

It was Arabella Warren.

"I am so sorry to disturb you this early, Miss Gray," she burst into speech. "But I'm driving back to Alexandria Bay today, to visit that poor lad Jonathan Van Camp and make sure the police haven't bullied him further or decided after all that he is responsible for that poor Mr. Gagne's death, or anything like that. I know, it's dreadful to keep using gasoline like this, but I can't sit at home and do nothing. I also want to know more about Mr. Gagne, if he has any family and what's being done about his funeral, because it seems to me we who inherited from Mr. Van Camp have a moral obligation if not a legal one to see to it he has one, a funeral, that is. I thought perhaps you would care to come with me, but if not I'll take myself off with apologies for disturbing you."

Pauline had intended to wash the dishes and sweep and dust, and then take the 10:30 train from Canton to Clayton, but this was far better. She relinquished her housework without regret.

"Let me leave a note for my friend and then I will be right with you," she said.

Sarah—gone with A.W. to Thousand Islands for the

day. Unsure when we'll return. For heaven's sake don't enable my slothfulness by doing my chores—I'll tend them when I get back. Good luck with Miss Nelson.

"Here is your paper, by the way," Miss Warren said, handing her the *Times*. "It was at the foot of the stairs as I came up. Your paper boy must be dreadfully sloppy."

Pauline agreed and thanked her with a nod while taking the paper.

Miss Warren sighed. "My father, God rest his soul, always said it was inappropriate for a lady to have her name in the paper for anything besides her birth, marriage, and death. Well, my name was in the *Times* last month because I was foolish enough to answer a reporter's questions about my opinion on the end of Prohibition, and I suppose it will be again if someone gets a hold of this story. Oh—not you, Miss Gray. I know you won't print anything without permission. I trust you, naturally. You're not just a reporter."

"Thank you," Pauline said, putting on hat and gloves and making sure her bag held a fresh notebook and enough sharpened pencils. "But I must warn you that I am planning on using a story for my column as an excuse to ask questions of the other heirs, in order to hopefully find a connection between you all that would tell us why Mr. Van Camp chose you. However, I will not use anyone's name without permission, including yours."

The air felt even more springlike today than yesterday; Pauline even saw the green spikes of some early crocuses out on various lawns as they flashed past in Miss Warren's auto. Perhaps more snow *was* coming, as the farmers insisted, but today held the promise of daffodils and sun rather than snow and clouds.

"I do feel sorry for that Van Camp boy, I tell you, and I wish he would let me give him the diamond necklace. I don't think I'd ever feel right about owning it, knowing it had been promised to him, especially after all he's been through."

Pauline had, after obtaining Jonathan's permission, shared his story with Miss Warren on the drive home the prior evening. It seemed to have been preying on the other woman's mind ever since.

"But then," Miss Warren mused, "if Mr. Van Camp changed his mind, would it be right for me to go against it? He might have found out something dreadful about Jonathan, but I must say he seems like a nice boy to me. Oh, a bit rude, of course, but I've never met a boy that age who isn't rude occasionally, and he has more reason than most, and he could be polite enough when he put his mind to it. Helped me out of the auto, remember, and that's more than many would do. It makes me feel downright ill, thinking about him having to make his way in the world like he has, without ever a bit of kindness or affection shown him, and no family besides a few half-sisters he hasn't seen since he was thirteen. A boy belongs in a family, not in a boarding house! I tell you I almost offered to bring him right home with us yesterday after the police finally let us go. It didn't seem right to leave him there at the door like a stray cat."

"Indeed," Pauline agreed.

"And I tell you something else, I do not agree with Mr. Ramsey. Oh—you weren't there for this part, you and Jonathan had left the office by then. He said that Jonathan reminded him of his clerk's brother, who caused the family so much trouble that Mr. Ramsey finally paid for him to go to Canada to spare the family any more disgrace. He thought he had done a fine and noble act, you could tell from how he spoke, but with the clerk right there! The poor man—the clerk, not Mr. Ramsey—just shriveled right into himself. Well, Mr. Ramsey plumed himself so much for his actions I could barely get a word in edgewise, but I spoke up all right when he started running down young Jonathan and making all sorts of unfounded accusations against him."

Pauline had tried to follow all this, but the endless flow of conversation left her dazed. "Mmm," was all she dared reply.

"I told him outright he had no business saying such things about that poor boy and making such accusations when he didn't know a thing about it, and I was there on business, not to listen to gossip! He changed his tune then, right sharp, got in a fine huff and said he never gossiped, and finally his secretary —you remember that Miss Peck?—had to intervene and calm him down, and that's when he finally gave me the necklace. He, I say, when really she was the one who opened the safe and removed the necklace, treating him like the petulant child he was acting.

And I must say, Miss Gray, I was a tiny bit disappointed in the necklace. Oh, it's beautiful all right—I meant to show it to you yesterday, but we were all so distracted by that poor Mr. Gagne's death, it didn't seem right—but somehow, I always thought there would be something more magical about a diamond necklace. This just looks like bits of glass. That's another reason I wouldn't mind giving it to Jonathan. It doesn't seem all that special. But there, he already said he wouldn't accept it, and I'm sure I don't know how to convince him to take it, he's that proud. What do you think?"

Thus adjured, Pauline had to force her mind back along the tortuous trail of Miss Warren's thoughts to find the original point.

"I don't know," she said, and braced herself for another spate of volubility.

It was going to be a long drive.

CHAPTER SEVEN

Complications

J ane Casper of Cape Vincent, NY, was only thirty-three, but discontentment had shaped her life such that she looked and sounded twenty years older. Her only satisfaction in life came from her award-winning cabbages, which, she informed Pauline, had won the blue ribbon at various fairs so many times the Cape Vincent Times had done a piece on it last month.

"And I consider that far more important than some inheritance which has nothing to do with me in the first place," she said. "That old Van Camp only left it to me because of my late brother."

Pauline pricked up her ears. "Really? Mr. Van Camp was acquainted with Mr. Casper?"

"What? No, of course not. The likes of him don't mingle with folk like us. I doubt that man ever set eyes on Elwin in his life."

"Then why ..."

"I'm telling you, aren't I? Listen: my brother Elwin Casper was a very important man here in Cape

Vincent."

Pauline longed to ask what award-winning vegetables he had grown, but she bit her tongue.

"He owned the general store, and everyone shopped there, and they came to ask his advice about everything in their lives even when they didn't need to buy anything. None of them ever paid any attention to *me*, mind you. But what can you expect?"

"But you said Mr. Van Camp never met your brother. How then would your brother have given him advice ...?"

"That ain't what I'm saying at all! Clearly, Van Camp had heard of my brother being one of Cape Vincent's most prominent citizens, and since Elwin had died, decided to instead leave his nearest relative— that's me—a token of appreciation for all he'd done for the town."

Pauline blinked at this convoluted logic. "That's ..."

"After all, why else would the man leave me something? I've certainly never met him. Barely even heard anything about him, only as that rich New Yorker who bought a place in Alex Bay. And this bracelet: great big thing with gaudy green stones all over it. Emeralds, the lawyer man called it, but I doubt it. Just big green pieces of glass, if you ask me. Nobody would leave me a real emerald bracelet, not for my brother's sake or anything."

"Maybe he heard of your cabbages and wanted you to have a proper award for them," Pauline said, and made her escape to the next house on the list.

Brian Nettleton was the eldest of five children, working as a farmer alongside his father, and utterly bewildered by the legacy of a small but lovely diamond ring.

"I'm walking out with a girl, but we ain't anywhere near getting hitched," he said. "What'm I supposed to do with this here ring?"

Pauline asked if he'd known Mr. Van Camp at all, and he returned the answer she was coming to expect: not even if they had passed each other on the street.

The third person on her list, David Anderson, was not at home. His tired-eyed wife, answering Pauline's knock with a baby on her hip and a toddler clinging to her skirt, sighed when Pauline explained her purpose and asked when he was likely to return.

"If I knew the answer to that, I'd be a happy woman. He spent the winter working up the river at a logging camp, came home a few weeks ago and left just a few days ago to look for more work downstate."

A faint memory of something Pauline had recently read stirred. "One of the nine local men who brought back their fallen comrade?"

One of Pauline's colleagues had covered that story, along with reporters from half a dozen other papers in the area. Many local men went up to Canada or to Maine as loggers during the winter, a way of earning enough money for their families to survive the long, cold, snowy season.

But logging was dangerous work, and tragedy had struck for one of them. He came home in a coffin, accompanied by an honor guard of sorts of his fellow local lumberjacks. The papers had played it up tremendously.

Mrs. Anderson passed a weary hand over her eyes. "Yes. Oh, how I wish he didn't have to do that sort of work! I spend every winter scared he won't come home, and then what'll me and the little ones do? When the clerk from that lawyer fellow came and told us that Mr. Van Camp had left David a pair of sapphire earrings, I was sure it was the answer to all our troubles. I told David we ought to sell the things and put the money right in the bank, but he said it had to be a mistake. The clerk insisted there was no mistake, but David took the earrings with him downstate to have them appraised by a jeweler. He says if they are cheap imitations we'll keep them, but if they're valuable then they were supposed to be left to some other David Anderson, so either way we won't see any money from them."

"I'll stop by in a few days to see if he had returned," Pauline said, cursing the inadequacy of words to convey her heartache at her own helplessness in the face of Mrs. Anderson's struggle.

Never knowing from day to day if your husband was alive, or if you were going to have enough money for the next day's groceries. Raising your children practically on your own because your husband had to be gone so often just to be able to make enough money to keep a roof over your heads. Always hoping for something better, but unable to trust it when it comes.

She found herself fiercely hoping that for this family, at least, there had been no mistake or underhanded dealings, and that this could be a turning point for them.

It had been a singularly unprofitable day for her. She had spent the entire morning interviewing people, and had gotten no further along in understanding why Mr. Van Camp had made out his will the way he did, or who Mr. X was, or if there even *was* a Mr. X.

Neither Jane Casper nor Brian Nettleton nor Mrs. David Anderson knew of each other or had ever met Mr. Van Camp. The closest connection was Mrs. Anderson knowing of Miss Casper's award-winning cabbages, as her mother complained every year of losing the blue ribbon to the sour spinster. Nor were any of them familiar with the other names on the list from Mr. Ramsey. It seemed safe to assume the rest followed the same pattern.

Twelve heirs, unknown to each other and their benefactor unknown to them. The supposed heir cut out of the will. The gardener, a witness to the will, removed from questioning. The butler, also a witness, dead.

It was a mess. Pauline couldn't made heads nor tails of it.

She considered asking her friend Lieutenant James Richardson of the Canton Police Department what he thought of it all, but upon reflection, decided to save him as a last resort. Involving James felt more official than the snooping she was doing thus far. He might not be able to help anyway, given the difference in jurisdictions.

Pauline checked her watch. She still had time before meeting Miss Warren for the ride back to Canton. She looked around and took her bearings. The Anderson house was not so far from the Van Camp estate. Pauline found her feet naturally turning in that direction.

She didn't expect to learn anything new at the estate, but she felt compelled to return all the same, to look around once more, undistracted by dead bodies and dismissive policemen. Perhaps there was something there that she had missed before, something that the police, in their insistence on Mr. Gagne's death as accidental, had overlooked as well.

It was worth checking.

Poor Mr. Gagne's body had been removed already, thank goodness. Pauline thought of Miss Warren's wish to do something for the man or his family, how easily she had taken on that responsibility and how quickly she had turned to compassion. Pauline's own instincts tended toward justice; she wasn't sure but that Arabella Warren's way was better.

For better or worse, this was her path. She couldn't change how she was made.

Since the police had declared Mr. Gagne's death accidental, nothing had been done to prevent access to the site. Pauline remembered Mr. Ramsey's words about the hospital wishing strangers to stay away, but she considered this matter more important.

Under normal circumstances, she would never

treat legal restrictions so cavalierly, but murder was beyond the normal way of things.

Pauline walked up the long driveway with only the faintest prickling of conscience, catching her breath all over again at the grandeur of the view. The clear, pale blue of the sky came down to meet the darker ribbon of the river, the wooded islands shining with a pale green light in the sun.

Patients who would be fortunate enough to have this as their convalescent home would find their path to recovery aided indeed by such a beautiful spot—so long as Mr. Gagne's ghost did not return to haunt them.

Pauline instinctively avoided the area where she had found the body as she searched the property, stopping and scolding herself for fastidiousness when she realized what she was doing. How could she expect to find anything of use if she wouldn't even examine the spot where he had died?

She told herself over a dozen times that she needed to overcome her folly and inspect the area, and over a dozen times she could not make her feet walk in that direction, exploring everywhere else instead—in vain.

At last, irritated and overheated, she stopped and rested by the shed housing Mr. Gagne's auto. Idly, she wondered what would happen to the vehicle now its owner was dead. At least cars weren't like horses; it could not be expected to miss its master, nor would anyone have to worry about feed or stabling. A roof to protect it from the elements and gasoline when you wanted to go somewhere, that was all an automobile required, as far as Pauline knew.

The black Ford was a handsome vehicle, gleaming darkly even in the shade of the enclosed shed. As she looked more closely, wondering if it was time to update Emma Daring's automobile in her stories, something glinted under the farther front tire, catching a shaft of sunlight slanting in through the open door.

Frowning, she peered more closely. The object, whatever it was, continued to catch the sunlight and reflect it back tantalizingly, but refused to be identified.

Impelled more by curiosity than anything else, Pauline crouched down by the tire and stretched a gloved hand out to the item. It took some scrabbling with her fingers, but at last she had it, hard and smooth and shaped like a small warped oval. She rose and opened her hand to examine her treasure.

Resting on the palm of her hand, nestled on the now rather dirty cream-colored glove, was a blue stone shaped like a teardrop, its facets sparkling like moving water in the weak spring sun.

Pauline knew only slightly more about jewels than she did about automobiles, but she was ready to swear this was a genuine sapphire.

What on earth was it doing here?

It had to be from the Van Camp collection; anything else was too much of a coincidence. But how? And why?

Mrs. Anderson's voice echoed in her ears: "... *left*

David a pair of sapphire earrings ...came home a few weeks ago ... left just a few days ago to look for more work ...”

Pauline curled her hand over the sapphire instinctively. No, no, no! Their mysterious Mr. X couldn't be David Anderson. How would he have known about the Van Camp collection? How could he have compelled Mr. Van Camp to change his will? And why would he have only taken one pair of earrings, if so, and then lost one of the jewels?

It wasn't logical. There had to be another explanation.

What if Mr. Gagne was a jewel thief? Perhaps he had stolen the sapphire? But then, why leave the jewelry at all to strangers, and how did he alter the will without the lawyer knowing?

Fragments of memory drifted through her mind. Arabella Warren, confessing her necklace wasn't as thrilling as she'd thought it would be. Jane Casper, insisting her emerald bracelet couldn't possibly be real.

What if Mr. Gagne had replaced the jewels in all the pieces with imitations? What if he had then forged a will, leaving those pieces to people he had come into contact with or heard of (but how?) throughout the region, people he thought unlikely to recognize the difference between a fake jewel and a real one? What if Mr. Van Camp had died without even knowing his will had been changed?

Pauline came up against a snag. The lawyer. Mr. Ramsey had been the one to make up the will for Mr.

Van Camp, so he would have known the original bequests. The current will couldn't be a forgery. Besides, now she thought of it, the jewelry had been in his possession as executor before he delivered it to the heirs, and she doubted he would be taken in by imitations.

No, her theory wouldn't hold water. In one way she was relieved.

If Mr. Gagne had been the villain, that would have left them with one obvious question: who killed him?

The answer was just as obvious: the dispossessed true heir, who had discovered the man had cheated his great-uncle and robbed him of his inheritance.

Jonathan Van Camp.

Pauline didn't want to believe the boy could be a killer any more than she'd wanted to believe David Anderson could be. She liked Jonathan, just as she'd pitied and admired Mrs. Anderson for her courage and endurance. Still, she knew that personal opinions held very little weight against logic and evidence. She was just as glad to have her theory fall apart.

None of that answered the burning questions at hand, which were: where had this sapphire come from, and what did it have to do with Mr. Gagne's death and the will?

Slipping the jewel into her handbag until she knew what to do with it, Pauline left the estate to walk back into town to meet Miss Warren.

She would ask the other woman to take her necklace to a jeweler and have it appraised, just in case there had been a switch, and she would phone Mrs. Anderson tomorrow to ask if her husband had contacted her with information about their sapphire earrings.

She would be glad if the small blue gem resting in her bag was the property of the Anderson family, all other questions and problems aside. They needed it even more than Miss Warren needed a neat and tidy solution to her problem.

CHAPTER EIGHT

The Second Murder

I
t was Arabella Warren who poked the first hole in Pauline's theory, on the drive back to Canton. Pauline had told the older woman her suspicions about the jewels being fake, though not about the sapphire she had found.

"Land's sake!" Miss Warren said. "Now, that's the first thing about this that has made sense. Mr. Van Camp must have switched the jewels himself!"

"Himself?"

"Say he lost money—so many have, you know, since that dreadful crash five years ago—and he needed to sell his jewels. But he didn't want to do without the pieces altogether, so he had them replaced with, oh, what do they call it? Paste, that's it." Her eyes sparkled. "And that's why he didn't leave the jewelry to Jonathan after all! He didn't want his great-nephew to discover he was a poorer man than he made himself out to be, so instead he left them to people who wouldn't notice or care about such things."

It was a logical explanation, and far simpler than the convoluted theories Pauline had concocted. The sapphire tucked in her bag, however, defied such a simple explanation.

"In any case, we should have your necklace checked," Pauline said. "Mr. MacPhee, perhaps?"

The sign on Mr. MacPhee's business on Main Street read "Jeweler and Optometrist," a combination that had always intrigued and amused Pauline, which was why his name stuck in her memory. In the general way of things, she had no need of a jeweler's services.

Miss Warren agreed, and that was all there was time for before she dropped Pauline off at the apartment on Pleasant Street. Pauline felt a pang of guilt for not inviting the woman to stay for dinner, but she could only take so much chatter in a day.

She knew she ought to be more gracious and hospitable, especially in the face of Miss Warren's loneliness, but guilty emotions could not overcome her deep reluctance to give up a peaceful evening.

Back inside, Pauline slipped on a yellow calico apron to protect her white blouse and navy skirt, and began work on her neglected chores. Sarah had not yet returned, so she had the apartment all to herself. The silence soothed her and helped to settle some of the unease stirred up by the day's events. As she swept, dusted, and washed dishes, Pauline felt the tension loosen from her neck and shoulders, and a mild headache she hadn't even realized was there faded away.

She did not love housework, but the act of bringing order out of chaos helped her feel more calm and regulated in her own mind and emotions. It was too easy to get wrapped up in the griefs and sorrows of other people, and fret over her inability to cure all the world's ills. Better than not caring about the world's ills at all, perhaps, but a type of hubris in its own way. Putting her own small household to rights; that was a good place to begin. Helping others to the extent of her abilities; another good step. Twisting herself into knots because she couldn't do everything; that was arrogance.

The apartment was sparkling and Pauline was standing in front of the cupboard, wondering what to prepare for supper, when Sarah came home.

"Oh, what a day," Sarah groaned, collapsing into her chair at the kitchen table.

A few hours ago, Pauline would have been so wrapped up in her need to solve the case she would have asked Sarah about Miss Nelson without so much as a thought for her friend's own difficult day. Now, she took one look at the weary lines etched into Sarah's face, bit her tongue, and poured her a glass of orange juice cool and sweet from the icebox.

"Recalcitrant patients?" she asked.

"Overbearing doctors and head nurses," Sarah said. She took a long drink. "Thank you. I needed that!"

Pauline freely admitted she wouldn't be able to do Sarah's job. She had neither the patience nor the sensibilities for nursing. She was often ashamed of her own fastidiousness in that way—a nurse was a far nobler profession than journalist or academic—but one thing college had taught her was that there was little point in kicking against the goads. All people were as they were made. God or nature had designed Pauline to be a scholar and a writer, just as Sarah had been designed to take care of sick people.

So long as they both used their gifts to make the world a better place, neither had anything to be ashamed of. All the same, Pauline thought her friend deserved far more accolades than anyone gave her.

"I'm afraid I didn't take the time to visit Miss Nelson," Sarah said now.

Pauline poured a second glass of juice and sat down across from her friend. "Never mind that. Out of all the people I have visited today, the only thing they had in common was having nothing in common. I can't imagine Miss Nelson would be any different."

Sarah sighed. "A fruitless day for you as well, then?"

Pauline thought of the sapphire weighing down her handbag. "Not exactly," she admitted with a wry twist to her mouth. "But that can wait until after supper. Just as soon as I think of what to prepare."

Sarah leaned out from her chair to study the contents of the cupboard past Pauline's figure partially blocking the open door.

"Potato soup," she said. "And while that's cooking, I'll make skillet biscuits and you can tell me what you mean by 'not exactly.' Would you make me wait to hear the answer to that riddle and spoil my meal on top of my dreadful day?"

Pauline laughed. As she awkwardly peeled and chopped potatoes and carrots for the soup, she built up the story of her day, from Miss Casper's sour outlook on life and Brian Nettleton's pleasant bewilderment to Mrs. David Anderson's weariness and fear. Sarah shook her head while she cut the lard into the flour mixture and added just the right amount of buttermilk without measuring

"All very well and good," she said, dropping dough into the cast iron skillet with a practiced hand. "But where's the 'not exactly fruitless' part?"

Pauline realized, as she tipped the vegetables into the pot and added water to cover them, that she was reluctant to tell Sarah about the sapphire. Taking it from the property had been, if not illegal, a reckless and improper move. The correct thing to have done would have been to leave it there and inform the police.

In this case, Pauline didn't think the correct move was the *right* one. But it was difficult to explain that.

"You did *what*?" Sarah said, closing the oven door with a bang. She whirled in a flurry of skirt to stare at her friend and roommate, mouth agape. "You stole a jewel! And brought it back home with you? It's sitting in your handbag by the door—what if we are robbed?"

"Nobody knows I have it, so no one would think to rob us," Pauline said, slightly defensive. "And it isn't stealing! I'm not keeping it for myself. It's a clue."

"Nevertheless, if you had to remove it from the crime scene, you should have taken it directly to Mr. Ramsey," Sarah said severely.

The knowledge that Sarah was right pricked Pauline's conscience, causing her to speak even more defensively than before. "I thought you believed Mr. Ramsey was the villain of the piece!"

"Whether he is or not, there is a way things should be done in a civilized society, and walking off with a jewel that does not belong to you is not that way."

It was the closest the two women had ever come to a true quarrel. They disagreed frequently, but not with the edge of temper that currently trembled beneath their words.

Pauline hated quarrels. She drew a long, steadying breath.

"Perhaps you are right," she forced herself to admit. "I was only thinking of the implications of my discovery, not of the correct procedure."

Sarah smoothed her hands down her skirt front. "I am going to change," she said.

By the time she returned with her face washed, her hair released from its tight bun to curl around her face, and her uniform changed for a pretty flowered house dress, the potatoes tested done to Pauline's fork and the biscuits were ready to be taken out of the oven.

Pauline added salt, a small amount of butter, and a splash of milk, stirred for a few more minutes, and pronounced the soup done.

The carrots were still crunchy and the broth was bland, but overall it wasn't bad, for one of Pauline's meals. Nothing had burnt, which was a pleasant change. The biscuits, of course, were perfect.

By unspoken consent, neither woman mentioned the quarrel or the case during the meal. It made for a fairly silent hour.

Dessert was chicory coffee and fruit cocktail made from canned fruit. Pauline's cooking skills may have been lacking, but nobody could have complained of her coffee making ability. With the first sip, Sarah's face finally relaxed.

"What are you going to do with the sapphire?" she asked.

Pauline accepted the olive branch. "Tomorrow I shall telephone Mrs. Anderson to inquire if her husband has returned with an answer from the jeweler. After that ... I am not certain. It depends on the answer, I suppose."

"I wish all this was happening in Canton instead of Clayton," Sarah said. "Then I could talk you into turning the case over to James."

"I wouldn't require much persuasion," Pauline said. "James would listen to my ideas. The Clayton police patted my head and sent me on my way when I told them my suspicions regarding Mr. Gagne's death. I cannot think they'd listen to me now."

Sarah giggled. "Sorry!" she said. "The image of you having your head patted by a nice stout police officer!"

They shared a burst of merry laughter, the

ice between them melting entirely. They took their coffees into the living room and listened to *Bing Crosby Entertains* on the radio before retiring, the evening ending on a far more pleasant note than it had begun.

The next morning Sarah left early for work, saying she might try to stop in and see Miss Nelson after her shift for the sake of completeness. After Pauline cleaned the breakfast detritus, she picked up the telephone and requested the number of the David Anderson family of Clayton, NY. Within a few moments, the line was ringing.

She didn't think anyone was going to answer at first, but as she was on the verge of hanging up, a harsh female voice broke on her ear.

"Who is this?"

Startled, Pauline tried to gather her scattered wits. "Is-is this Mrs. Anderson?" she stammered, then pulled herself together. Really, she hadn't stammered since high school!

"No, it ain't," said the other woman aggressively. "What do you want with her?"

"My name is Pauline Gray, and I hoped—"

"Pauline Gray! I've heard of you. You're that newspaper woman. You vultures, you're all alike. Can't you even let a woman grieve in peace before breaking in with your poking and prying?"

"I don't understand," Pauline said, gripping the receiver hard enough to turn her knuckles white, the familiar nausea of an unexpectedly unpleasant situation churning in her stomach.

The woman snorted, causing Pauline to jump as the sound attacked her ear. "We don't want no reporters here. Good bye!"

She slammed the receiver down, making Pauline jump yet again.

"What," Pauline said aloud as she carefully replaced the receiver on the base, positioning it ever-so-precisely in place, "was that about?"

As if in answer to the conundrum, the telephone rang.

By now Pauline's nerves were too numbed for her to jump again. She simply picked it up and said, "Hello?"

"Miss Gray?" The voice was eerie in its calmness; it was a voice lacking all emotion or life. So might a dead person speak, Pauline's imagination whispered before she forced it down.

"Yes. Who is this, please?"

"Barbara Anderson ... Mrs. David Anderson." The woman stopped and cleared her throat. "I apologize for earlier ... my neighbor took your call, she didn't understand ... Miss Gray, please, do you know anything about my husband's death?"

"Death?"

Pauline's head spun. "I had no idea," she gasped, reaching out blindly with her free hand for support. Her grasping fingers found the edge of the telephone cabinet and held on for dear life. "I'm so sorry—of course I wouldn't have intruded upon your grief if I'd known."

"Oh." A note of disappointment entered the

woman's flat tone. "I thought—I thought maybe you knew something about it. The police insist on treating it as a robbery that got out of hand, but ... it doesn't fit. It doesn't make sense, Miss Gray. I thought, since you were here asking questions yesterday, that maybe you had information ... knew something the police don't."

"I don't have real information," Pauline said, reason slowly returning. "Not that I'm aware of. But if you wouldn't mind telling me what happened, I might ..." She caught her breath at the brazen audacity of what she was saying. How dare she take this on her shoulders, promise anything to this woman, give her false hope?

But if her suspicions were correct, did she dare do nothing? Wasn't that her responsibility—not to promise results, but to at least try? For Mr. Anderson as much as for Mr. Gagne?

Mrs. Anderson took the matter out of her hands. "My husband was murdered," she said, her voice ringing emptily along the line. "Last night or early this morning, as he was returning from his trip downstate. He was robbed and killed—"

Her voice gave out.

"That is dreadful," Pauline said. "I'm so very sorry." She knew she was repeating herself, but what else could one say?

The neighbor's voice came back in response. "That's enough of that!" she said. "Didn't ought to be upsetting her like this, as any decent woman would know. You career women, you've no sense of what's proper."

"I *am* sorry," Pauline said. "Believe it or not, I am trying to help. I am glad you came back on the line —I don't want to ask Mrs. Anderson this. Can you tell me, please, how Mr. Anderson was killed?"

"Not the sort of thing a young woman ought to be asking," snapped the neighbor. "Ghoul!"

"I am not asking for my own curiosity, I assure you," Pauline said.

Muffled noise in the background suggested Mrs. Anderson was requesting her neighbor cooperate.

"Head bashed in with a rock," she finally came back with.

The same method as was used for Mr. Gagne.

"And Mrs. Anderson wants me to tell you that her husband was a God-fearing man who wouldn't have gone into a drinking place, temperance laws done away with or no, much less gotten so tipsy as to brag about them earrings, neither."

"Is that what the police think happened?"

"Seems to be. They found the—him outside one of them devil-places, and it's a shame Prohibition ever ended if you ask me! His pockets were emptied, and they say someone must have heard him talking about his good fortune and decided to take that fortune for their own. But Mrs. Anderson says her husband wouldn't have done that, and not that it's any of your business, but I agree with her. I haven't lived next door to them for ten years without learning something about who they are!"

"Thank you," Pauline said, ignoring the

woman's tone and responding instead to the information. "I have only one more question and then I will leave you in peace. I need the name and telephone number of the jeweler Mr. Anderson was going to consult."

The neighbor relayed the request and reeled the information back off to Pauline. Then Mrs. Anderson came back on, her voice showing some signs of life.

"Miss Gray—you believe me."

"I do," Pauline said.

"You do know something about how this happened."

"There's a chance it is connected to a much larger matter, yes," Pauline said cautiously. "I can't say anything for certain."

"I want the culprit found and my husband's reputation restored," the new widow said. "You must find out the truth and publish it, Miss Gray. Please."

There was no answer Pauline could give but, "I will do my best."

After hanging up she dialed the number of the jeweler quickly, before she stopped to think about it. She couldn't fall to pieces now.

It took some persuading for the jeweler to reveal the information to her. She finally had to tell him she was a private detective employed by Mrs. Anderson to discover who had murdered her husband, which wasn't even that much of a stretch of the truth, before he, uttering little cries of shock and horror at the news of Mr. Anderson's death, would share customer information.

The news was as Pauline had expected, but gave her a jolt nonetheless. "The gems in the earrings were paste," the jeweler said. "Well done, but not clever enough to fool an expert even for a moment. Why, I doubt they would have stood up even against the eye of a woman accustomed to jewels, or that of a man buying them for her. I didn't even have to touch them to know the difference."

Pauline was acutely aware of the small blue stone still in her handbag. "What shape were they?"

"Teardrops. Exquisite Classical Revival pieces, you know, designed to resemble the shape of an amphora. What I wouldn't give to see them set with their true stones! A rare and lovely set originally."

"Thank you," Pauline said, and replaced the receiver.

Only then did she allow herself to give in to her shaking legs and sit down.

Another death. Another murder. This proved it. Mr. Gagne's death was no accident. This was no coincidence.

Sarah's question from the previous evening hung before Pauline's eyes as clearly as though the words were printed in the air.

What was she going to do now?

CHAPTER NINE

Danger on the Road

The next step, Pauline decided, was finding out if Arabella Warren had taken her necklace to Mr. MacPhee yet. Exerting her will to control the trembling still affecting her hands, she reached for the telephone once again.

Before she could pick up the receiver, someone knocked on the door. This proved to be Miss Warren herself, looking even more flustered than usual.

"Oh good, Miss Gray. Mr. Ramsey's office telephoned, they have some papers they need me to sign and they need the necklace as well. I don't understand why, that clerk mumbles so, and would you mind coming with me? Even when they speak clearly I don't understand all that legal talk, and I'd rather have someone there who could tell me what it is I'm signing."

"Of course," Pauline said, stifling a sigh. Yet another auto ride to Clayton. Like Sarah, though for different reasons, Pauline wished this affair was taking place in Canton. "Have you had a chance to have the necklace evaluated yet?"

"Goodness no, I've far too much to do in the mornings. At least, I don't need to do everything I do —making bread each day is silly when I'm the only one at home, but my neighbors seem to appreciate the extra loaves, and scrubbing my floors sometimes seems futile when nobody ever stops by to visit, but you know how it is, you get into the habit of doing something and you can't seem to stop even when it's no longer necessary."

Pauline didn't understand this at all, but she smiled and nodded before fetching her hat, gloves, and handbag. As a precaution, she transferred the sapphire into an old pillbox and tucked it into the drawer of her nightstand. Not that she expected to be robbed, but it was only sensible to not carry that much wealth on her person, especially when it was also an important clue and didn't belong to her in the first place.

"Lunch in town before we go," Miss Warren declared as they left the apartment, Pauline carefully locking the door behind her. "Mr. Ramsey may want me there as soon as possible, but he will have to accept that we must eat."

She took Pauline to the Hotel Harrington grill, even as Pauline protested it was far too expensive. Canton's only hotel was terribly posh; Pauline wouldn't have dreamed of eating there on her own.

"Nonsense," Miss Warren said. "Miss Gray, I am not a wealthy woman, although I suppose if the diamonds in my new necklace are real I am now, but

I never have been wealthy, and yet I've always had more than enough for one person to live comfortably. I've no children to spend it on, the least I can do is treat a friend once in a while to a nice meal."

Put like that, Pauline could only be ashamed of her reluctance to accept such an expensive treat, and respond with as much grace as possible. She also agreed to the other woman's proposition that they dispense with "Miss" and use each other's given names. It was a step toward intimacy Pauline wasn't entirely comfortable with, but she could not see a way to refuse that wouldn't have sounded snobbish or churlish.

The dining room was an elegant, airy space, lit by electricity, with tables laid with white linen cloths and deft waiters to attend to the diners' every whim. For a few dizzying moments, Pauline was transported to her childhood, when outings like this were common. She had never thought of her family as wealthy—did not her mother complain constantly of not having enough money? After the stock market crash of '29 they had had to tighten their belts along with the rest of the business world, causing Mrs. Gray to moan even more about hard times.

Living in a rural community and supporting herself on her own wages had opened Pauline's eyes considerably. Not only had her family at their poorest had more money than most folks in Canton who were considered well-off, they had led a tremendously sheltered life. Poverty and hard work alike were closed books to Pauline's mother, as to Pauline herself when she had first moved here.

Her own experiences and her friendships with the people of Canton had begun the process of change. She was honest enough to admit she still had a long way to go.

For all that, even with the melancholia that still gripped her at times, Pauline had no regrets about exchanging her former life for this one. She appreciated and enjoyed the luxury of a meal such as the elegant shrimp salad and soft dinner roll now served to her, but as a step outside her everyday life, not as a matter of course.

Even the novels which she could not help but be somewhat ashamed of writing were an honest source of income, not inherited or gotten on the backs of other people. They might not have been the scholarly works she dreamed of someday penning, but she could take pride in them as the work of her own hands.

The meal was prepared to perfection, and both Arabella and Pauline were mellowed as they finally took to the road after finishing with coffee and ices. Arabella was less talkative than usual, and Pauline felt comfortable enough to share some college stories with her.

"This makes me think of the time Katie Holtman borrowed her father's auto and took several of us on a drive to the river one April," she said. "She forgot to fill it with gasoline so we were stranded by the side of the road for hours until a sympathetic farmer came along and gave us enough to come sheepishly back to campus." She laughed. "We never let Katie live it down, but it became one of my favorite memories, all of the jokes we made and songs we sang while stranded."

"I would have liked to go to college, but my father considered it nonsense. Not because I was a woman, but he said my mind wasn't serious enough. I'm sure he was right, but still I can't help but feel wistful when I think about it. Everyone seems to have such wonderful memories of their time there." Arabella sighed, steering around a gentle bend in the road.

"I think—Oh!" Pauline cried out as Arabella applied the brake suddenly. They were jolted forward in their seats and the auto skidded with a squeal of tires, coming to a halt inches before the brown trunk of an uprooted young ash tree that lay flung across the road.

"Goodness!" Pauline said once she'd caught her breath.

"How on earth did this end up here?" Arabella asked. "There hasn't been any sort of windstorm or rain."

"More importantly, what are we going to do about it?" Pauline said. "I doubt the two of us together are strong enough to remove it."

"Well, we certainly can't do anything by sitting here," Arabella said briskly.

She maneuvered the auto to the side of the road, put it in park, and opened the door to step out. Pauline admired her prompt decision and followed suit, slightly ashamed of her instinct to sit and wait for someone else to take care of the problem.

"If we had some rope, we could try tying one end to the tree and one end to your bumper, and you could drive ..." she began, thinking of what Emma Daring, the dauntless heroine of her novels, would do. Her voice faltered as Arabella shook her head.

"A tractor or a truck would be strong enough for that, but I fear it would only rip my bumper clean off," she said. "Oh," in a different tone, turning her head to look up the road. "Oh, do be careful! Look out!" she called, waving both hands.

The bicyclist approaching at full speed, warned by her cry, slowed to a stop well before hitting the tree. It was Jonathan Van Camp.

"Whew!" he whistled. He swung his leg over the bar of the bicycle, climbed down and leaned the machine against the bank, then walked over to look at the tree trunk. "This is a mess, isn't it? What on earth are you doing here?"

"We are on our way to Mr. Ramsey's office," Pauline answered. "What are you doing?"

He shrugged. "Oh, you know. Here, step back. I can shift this, no sense you two dirtying your gloves."

He flashed a cheeky grin at them before taking hold of the branches at one end and heaving the tree to one side and pushing it off the road.

Pauline wouldn't be distracted. She might not be much use in practical matters, but she knew when someone was evading a question.

"No, I don't know," she said. "What brings you

down this road at the precise right time for us?"

A new voice rang out behind them.

"Stop! Hands up!"

Arabella Warren screamed. Pauline spun around.

A masked figure had appeared out of the woods lining the road, an ugly black gun in one hand.

"You—ladies—give me your handbags," he demanded.

A trap! The tree had been put across the road on purpose to stop their car and force them to get out into the open. Pauline exchanged a glance with Arabella.

The diamond necklace was in the other woman's bag. If they let him have it, they would lose their chance to have it identified as paste or real.

But it wasn't worth their lives. Pauline nodded, and turned back to the auto to take out their bags.

"Toss them to him," Jonathan said in a low, urgent voice. "Make him bend down to pick them up."

Pauline grasped the point at once. Of course! It was just what Emma Daring would do. Dangerous and terribly foolhardy, of course, but she trusted Jonathan's reflexes.

She tossed the bags toward the masked figure. They landed with a rattle before his feet, and just as she had hoped, he bent over to reach for them. Jonathan jumped onto the tree trunk and launched himself at the man. It was an unorthodox method, but it worked.

The would-be thief crashed to the ground,

dropping his gun as he did, Jonathan on his back and swinging wildly. The boy hit dirt as often as he made contact with any part of the man's anatomy, but his position gave him the advantage. The other man could do nothing but attempt to throw him off.

Arabella screamed again as she watched the two scuffling on the ground, the thief trying to throw Jonathan off, Jonathan trying equally hard to keep the thief down. Pauline's heart was pounding erratically, her lower lip caught tightly between her teeth. She longed to help, but knew she would be more of a liability than an actual asset to Jonathan.

Arabella's third scream took on a more panicked note as the masked man made one final, desperate heave and flung Jonathan off long enough to reclaim his gun and scramble to his feet. He fired wildly into the air, then turned and fled back into the woods.

Uninjured, Jonathan scrambled to his feet and prepared to chase after him. Arabella rushed forward and grabbed his arm.

"Don't you dare! That horrible man will kill you!"

"But he's getting away!" Jonathan protested, tugging at his sleeve to free it.

Pauline scooped the handbags back up. "Let him," she advised. "He didn't get what he came for. This is now a matter for the police. Miss Warren is right, Jonathan. If you chase him, he's bound to shoot you."

The boy stopped struggling. "Very well," he muttered. "But I could have had him."

"You were enough of a hero as it was!" Arabella exclaimed. "Goodness, when I think what would have happened to us if you weren't here. It was positively providential!"

"Er ... yes," Jonathan said, eyes shifting.

"We need to get to Clayton to report this as soon as possible," Pauline said. "But first, Jonathan, stop avoiding the matter. It wasn't Providence that brought you here, was it?"

His shoulders sagged. "No," he mumbled. "Got a note—pushed under my landlady's door—not signed. Told me to be here at this time if I wanted to know what really happened with my uncle's will."

Curiouser and curiouser.

They tucked Jonathan and his bicycle somehow into the back of the auto and drove off again, arriving at Mr. Ramsey's office at last.

"But, my dear lady, I never telephoned you! No, nor had George do so," the lawyer protested once he understood their jumbled tale. "Not but what I'm delighted to see you at any time, and Miss Gray as well, but no, I have no papers for you to sign. And I never would have asked you to bring back the necklace! As I told you when I entrusted it to your care, it ought to be in the bank."

He mopped his forehead with a scarlet handkerchief held in trembling fingers. "This is dreadful news about the attempted robbery, simply dreadful. George ... oh that's right, he's checking the status of his paintings with the post office. He's an amateur artist, you know, and he recently sent three of his best paintings off to be framed, and he wants to be certain the postman understands that when they return they must be delivered here for safekeeping, not his boarding house, where his landlady has no respect for other people's property ... but you aren't interested in that! Eleanor—you all remember Miss Peck, my secretary —we must telephone to the police."

"Of course," the secretary murmured in her dampening way. "I only hope they'll take it seriously."

"Seriously?" Arabella shrilled. "We were nearly killed! If Jonathan hadn't been there we would have been. How could they not take that seriously?"

Miss Peck's smile was a masterwork of condescension. "How fortunate young Mr. Van Camp was there so opportunely, then."

Arabella drew in a breath, but Pauline stepped on her foot. Light had dawned.

Had she and Arabella not delayed to eat luncheon, they would have been on the road much sooner, and Jonathan would have arrived at the tree block after they had already been robbed, placing him in the vicinity of the attack in a highly suspicious position. Would the police have believed his story of an anonymous note? Even if he could produce it, they might have thought he'd faked it himself as an alibi.

No, the more she thought about it, the more convinced she was that the note had been sent to set Jonathan up, to make it appear as though he were the one to rob Arabella in an attempt to steal back his great-uncle's jewels.

How lucky, how very lucky indeed, that Arabella had insisted on a proper meal before setting out! It was, as Miss Warren would have said, providential.

Pauline returned to the present to realize Mr. Ramsey was addressing her.

"Now, I'm sure this is a rare opportunity for you, Miss Gray, eh? Not every day a newspaper woman gets to be the subject of a story instead of the author of it, ha!"

Pauline considered the joke to be in extremely bad taste. "I'm afraid this is outside my purview, sir. I write a regular column. I am not a reporter."

"Oh! Well now, I didn't know it. I don't ever read the papers, myself. At least, not anymore. Too, ah, too busy, yes, far too busy. My dear Eleanor reads them all instead and tells me the bits she knows I'd be interested in. I'd be lost without her, yes indeed I would!"

Miss Peck, now on the telephone with the police, smiled coolly at this paean of praise.

Pauline had never known any man, much less one in the legal profession, who did not read at least one paper. It couldn't be considered a character flaw, but despite herself, her opinion of Mr. Ramsey dropped another notch all the same.

"Make sure she shares with you the tragic story of poor Mr. David Anderson in tomorrow's paper," she couldn't resist saying now. "He was murdered late last night or early this morning, and the sapphire earrings he inherited from Mr. Van Camp were stolen."

Mr. Ramsey's face lost all color. He dropped his

handkerchief. "What? No! My dear, you must be mistaken. Why, I saw him myself, yesterday afternoon."

Pauline hadn't realized he'd been out of town. "I'm sorry," she said, softening her tone a trifle. "But it's quite true. Mrs. Anderson told me herself."

"Oh dear, oh dear," the little man moaned. He reached for his forehead, seemed to realize he had no handkerchief, and looked around helplessly for it. Jonathan, who had been standing quietly in the background all this time, picked it up off the floor and handed it to the distraught lawyer.

"We were at a conference for the Bar Association in Utica yesterday, George, Eleanor, and myself, and we bumped into Mr. Anderson at a restaurant during our lunch break. Such a pleasant, well-spoken man. He told us he was having the earrings evaluated, which I thought extremely sensible of him, to get an idea of how much they were worth. And now they are stolen and he is murdered! Dear, oh dear."

Arabella's face was pale as well. "First Mr. Anderson, and today us. Somebody wants very badly to get those jewels."

Miss Peck replaced the receiver and folded her hands together on her desk. "Yes," she agreed quietly. "So it seems."

She looked directly at Jonathan.

"The police are on the way," she added.

Arabella Warren was not a subtle woman, but not even she could miss that implication. She scowled at the secretary. "Those thieves will be sorry when they find out the jewels they are stealing are only paste!"

Pauline would rather have held that information to herself until they had confirmation of the necklace being paste as well as the earrings, but she could not blame Arabella for spilling their suspicion. She hadn't told the other woman to keep it a secret. Now that it was out, she set herself to studying the others' reactions.

Mr. Ramsey's jaw dropped. George-the-clerk chose that moment to return; he tripped on the lintel and nearly fell into the office. Jonathan stared blankly at Arabella. Only Miss Peck remained unmoved by the announcement, raising a supercilious eyebrow.

"That is a very serious accusation, ma'am!" exclaimed Mr. Ramsey. "They most certainly are not paste! Dear, dear, what is the world coming to?"

CHAPTER TEN

An Unpleasant Afternoon

"**M**y great-uncle despised paste jewelry!" Jonathan exclaimed. "He would never have sold his jewels, never, no matter how poor he got in other ways. He wasn't poor, not at all, but if he had been, he still would have kept his jewels. The only way the collection could be paste would be if someone here, in this office, stole the real jewels after Great-Uncle Horace died. I knew you were a thief!" he finished up, glaring at Mr. Ramsey.

The little lawyer did not take that well. He insisted that the jewels were real when Mr. Van Camp showed them to him and George at the house, weren't they, George, and they were real when they arrived at his office, because Eleanor's cousin who was a jeweler had stopped in that day to take her to lunch and had commented favorably on their quality, didn't he, Eleanor, and the only way they could be false now was if someone had broken into his office while the will was in probate and swapped them, now what did Jonathan have to say to that?

"If," Jonathan said between his teeth, "you are implying that I did such a thing, I ask where your proof is."

"It makes perfect sense!" the lawyer insisted. "You remember, Eleanor, and you, George, the papers that were disarranged on my desk the day after Mr. Van Camp's death? We finally determined it must have been the breeze from opening the inner door at the same time someone closed the outer door, but now I see it all. You must have come in and broken into the safe, swapped the jewels, and left in the night!"

Pauline had to interrupt at this staggering leap of illogic. "Oh come, Mr. Ramsey. Where would Jonathan learn to break into a safe? Not to mention that such a deed would involve breaking the lock on your front door as well, and yet the only sign left behind was a few mussed papers?"

"Don't tell me about criminals, young lady, I know more about them than a sheltered, gently-brought up young woman like yourself ever could! There are thieves who can break any lock without leaving a trace, and many of them started younger than this fellow here. Isn't that right, George?"

This seemed an odd choice to back him up, as the unfortunate clerk blushed bright red and mumbled something at his shoes.

Arabella gasped. "Mr. Ramsey, you aren't saying your clerk was a thief?"

"Not at all, my dear lady, not at all. Apologies, George. Didn't mean to imply anything. I know it's a sore spot. His brother, ladies. He was a bad egg—no, I'm sorry George, at this point I have to tell them, can't leave them thinking it's you. Had to ship this brother off to Canada before he brought the Norton family name into any more disgrace. And I've seen a look in this young man's eye that reminds me very much indeed of M—"

It was perhaps fortunate that the police entered at this point, or Mr. Ramsey might have been able to charge Jonathan with assault.

Between Arabella Warren's incoherent account, Mr. Ramsey's not-veiled-at-all accusations of Jonathan as a scoundrel and rogue, Jonathan's scornful attitude, and the secretary's usual dampening effect on the room, Pauline's quiet and well-ordered rendering of the tale was lost. After an excruciating half hour, the police left once more, leaving behind the impression that they looked on the entire affair as nothing more than a prank.

"Now then," Mr. Ramsey said the instant the door closed behind the officers, "What exactly makes you think the jewels are paste, Miss Warren? After all, we must look as this in an orderly and logical fashion, mustn't we. Wouldn't do to lose our heads."

Pauline was under the impression that was exactly what had happened, but she was thankful the man was behaving as a member of the legal profession ought, however belated.

"Well, Pauline says that Mr. Anderson's earrings were paste, and she thinks the rest are as well ..." Arabella began.

Curiously enough, it was George who responded to that, not Mr. Ramsey. "Miss Gray, that is a highly serious accusation to make based on what seems to be the flimsiest of bases. I trust you have more to go on than women's intuition?"

"Ha!" said Mr. Ramsey. "Well put, George. Yes indeed. Women's intuition, not allowable in the courtroom, is it?"

Pauline's grasp on her temper had been tenuous at best through the interview with the police, and now it slipped entirely. "I learned at my grandfather's knee what was allowable and what was not in a court of law, thank you sir," she said icily. "At this time and in this place, I prefer to keep my conclusions, and the facts that led me to draw them, to myself."

Mr. Ramsey's eyes bulged. "Your grandfather ... good grief, Miss Gray, not Judge *Arthur* Gray, surely? Goodness gracious me. Yes indeed. Well, well, well. No wonder you are so familiar with legal procedures, yes indeed. If we'd known, we could have had Miss Gray draw up the will for Mr. Van Camp, eh George? Saved you the effort!" He chortled, seemingly under the impression he had made a statement of great wit.

George's smile was sickly. "Yes sir ... sir, it is getting late, and if Miss Gray refuses to share any more information with us, perhaps we should close for the evening?"

"Oh yes, naturally. Well, Miss Warren—"

"One moment," Pauline said. "Did you say your clerk drew up the will?" She wished Mr. Ramsey had introduced him properly. She still didn't know

LOUISE BATES

George's last name, but it would be too insolent to call him "George" as Mr. Ramsey did, leaving her with no option but the awkward "your clerk."

"Standard procedure, young lady, standard procedure! Your grandfather would have told you the same. All perfectly legal and in order. Van Camp had his list of bequests already written out. He handed it to me, I looked at it and saw that everything was in order, and passed it along to George with instructions to put it into the proper form for a will. While he was doing that, Van Camp showed me his jewelry collection along with the paintings he had collected, very fine they were. Then we came back into the room, Van Camp inspected the will, agreed that it was just as he wanted it, and went to the window to call the gardener in as a witness while I went into the hall to fetch the butler. Now, I know what you're going to ask next: don't worry, George covered up the actual bequests of the will so the witnesses wouldn't see it as they were signing."

Miss Peck spoke up again, startling them all with her smooth, spiteful voice. "Perhaps Miss Gray would like to view the will herself, as she seems to think something was improper in its formation?"

Mr. Ramsey drew himself up once more. "Improper!"

"It seems she has taken issue with George," Miss Peck continued. "Perhaps she thinks that because his brother is untrustworthy, he is as well."

"That is a highly regrettable attitude to take, Miss Gray, and not one worthy of your illustrious grandfather," Mr. Ramsey said, his tone indicating more sorrow than anger.

Pauline was too furious to speak. Arabella rescued her.

"Rubbish! Pauline said nothing of the kind. That is a ridiculous accusation. I am sure she never even thought such a thing for a moment. She was merely taking an interest in how it all happened, trying to get a picture of it, as anyone might want to do. For my part, I am honestly disappointed you saw the jewels and are certain they were real before Mr. Van Camp died, Mr. Ramsey, as I had so hoped he had switched them out himself. Then all this would make much more sense and we wouldn't have to have all this fuss. I am sure that was all Pauline was trying to ascertain, isn't that so?"

"Certainly I have no wish to imply impropriety in any of your or your clerk's actions in the writing of the will," Pauline agreed, her voice cold. Much as she loathed physical violence, her palm tingled with the urge to slap Miss Eleanor Peck.

"And now I think we'll leave," Arabella said. "Nothing else is going to get solved today, not with everybody so worked up. Jonathan, I hope you'll come with us."

The young man had been standing in the corner in surly silence ever since the police left. Now he stirred. "I'll need to get food somewhere. My landlady will have stopped serving supper by now."

Arabella patted his arm. "You come home with me, young man. I don't feel safe on the road or in my home without a man around, goodness me, not after that robbery attempt. I can guarantee you that my cooking will be better than a cold supper at your landlady's, even if I say so myself! I do enjoy cooking, but it always seems a waste for only me. It will be a real treat to feed a growing boy."

The quality of Jonathan's stillness changed from that of a boy disgusted by the scene he had been forced to witness, to a wild animal not sure whether or not to flee from an open hand held out to it.

"You want me to come to your home? Have a meal?"

"A meal, a bed ... I am asking you if you'd be willing to stay at my house, at least until this matter is cleared up. Only if you want to, of course."

Jonathan licked his lips. "I'll need to let my landlady know," he croaked.

"Of course," Arabella hurried to say. "Pauline and I don't mind stopping by there. I'm sure you'll want to pick up your things, anyway."

A genuine smile broke over Jonathan's face. "Don't have that much to collect."

"Miss Warren—dear lady—do stop and think for a moment," Mr. Ramsey pleaded. "You know nothing of this boy! You could be taking a criminal into your home!"

The smile vanished from Jonathan's face. Arabella placed one hand on his shoulder and faced Mr. Ramsey with eyes flashing.

"That's enough of that nonsense, Mr. Ramsey! This boy saved us from a robbery earlier today, and even if he hadn't, I'm just about tired of accusations without any basis but your own dislike. Jonathan is coming home with me, and that's that. Good evening."

Mr. Ramsey looked as though he wanted to protest further, but Pauline was as fed up as Arabella, in her own way. She stalked to the door with the barest of courtesies to the three remaining. Jonathan leapt in front to open the door for her, and she and Arabella swept through.

"Well!" Arabella said once they were all safely in the auto. "That was a most unpleasant way to spend the afternoon."

Pauline couldn't have agreed more.

CHAPTER ELEVEN

Unraveling Tangles

A stranger might have been forgiven for thinking Lieutenant James Richardson of the Canton Police Department was all brawn and no brains, for he was big and sturdy, and kept an easygoing grin on his face most of the time. Pauline knew better. James had a sharp mind and a keen wit, and he was not intimidated by clever women.

At times, his friendship with Pauline had given rise to local gossip, but his recent marriage to a young widow with one son had put an end to those rumors, much to Pauline's relief.

She liked James, no more and no less. She couldn't imagine feeling romantic about him—or about anyone, for that matter. But that was neither here nor there.

More relevant to the matter at hand, he took her seriously when she came into the police station on the first floor of the Opera House the morning after the attempted robbery, sat down in front of his desk, and told him the entire tale, from her first meeting with Arabella—arranged by his own wife—to the exit from Mr. Ramsey's office the previous evening. She set the list of names of the heirs down on his desk, so he could see it for himself rather than trying to keep it all straight in his head.

She even told him about finding the sapphire and taking it home with her, though not without an inward qualm about his reaction toward such law-lessness.

James didn't say anything the entire time aside from the occasional, "mm-hm." His face showed neither skepticism nor acceptance. The neutral expression was cultivated, Pauline knew, and went a long way toward unnerving criminals and subordinates alike.

"Well," he said when she finished. "This is a fine mess, isn't it?"

"That is one way to describe it," Pauline acknowledged with a wry smile. "But what do you make of it all, James?"

He rubbed his square, clean-shaven jaw. "I'm surprised you're asking me at all. I've never known you to rely on a man to tell you what to do."

Prickled, Pauline snapped, "Nonsense! You have been a policeman for several years, and this is only the second criminal matter I've ever investigated. Me coming to you is no different than a student asking a professor for advice on a difficult paper."

He laughed. "I'm sorry, I shouldn't tease you. And in truth, I'm flattered you are including me in this. I'll try to live up to your good opinion of me."

Pauline smoothed her skirts, regretting her outburst. She ought to have known better. James was a good friend, but he did love to tease, especially when it came to women's rights. It never failed to get under her skin.

"It's not my jurisdiction, you know," James said, tapping his fingers on the desk top. "And a good thing for you, or I'd have to report you for taking that sapphire."

"I know I shouldn't have done it," Pauline admitted. "Sarah is quite correctly unhappy with me for it as well. I would say that I don't know what came over me, except I do: I didn't—and still don't—trust anyone else involved to handle this matter properly. Mr. Ramsey is a fool, if I may be blunt, and the Thousand Islands police refuse to believe any of this is connected or significant. Until I know for certain who should have the sapphire, my conscience won't allow me to simply hand it off."

"You and your conscience," James muttered, but he accompanied the words with a faint grin. Pauline gathered he wasn't going to scold her too sharply over her peccadillo.

"I'm not asking you to involve yourself professionally—though I suppose I ought not to have come bothering you with a personal matter while you were on duty. I simply don't know where to go next with this. Miss Warren and Jonathan are taking the necklace to Mr. MacPhee this morning, and I am absolutely certain he will say the diamonds are paste. But even so, what then? What is the next step?"

James tapped his fingers again, noticed what he was doing, and quickly moved his hand off the desk. "It's true there are a lot of pieces that don't add up, and something is clearly amiss here. The trouble it, I don't have any right poking my nose into a case that is so clearly centered in the Thousand Islands, any more than they would be justified in interfering in our affairs here."

"I don't suppose the attempted robbery of two Canton citizens counts?" Pauline asked as a forlorn hope.

"Not for getting involved officially, but I will use that as my excuse if the chief asks me what I'm doing. After all, we can't have you running around getting yourself shot at—nor Miss Warren either."

"Believe me, I will be quite happy if I never in my life see another weapon pointed at me," Pauline said fervently.

"I should hope so."

Pauline waved her hand to dismiss the subject. No sense in dwelling on what had already happened, when they couldn't change the past. "So what do you think?"

"I think your best chance would be to catch your Mr. X in an act so blatant the police have to acknowledge it," James said. "A written confession would be best, obviously."

"Mr. X? Then you don't have one suspect you favor over another?"

Pauline ought to have been glad there wasn't something so obviously pointing to one suspect that only a rank amateur such as herself could have over-looked it, but she was disappointed. It would have been nice to have James see something right away that solved everything. She found herself getting increasingly tired of this case. For very little, she would have handed it over to the police and retired to her desk and typewriter.

"I'm with Sarah, I'd like it to be the lawyer. Unfortunately, I also agree with you that he seems highly unlikely, as he doesn't get anything out of the new will."

"But the paste jewels ... what if he stole the real jewels?"

"He still couldn't have altered the will to leave the false jewels to other people," James countered. "His clerk did the actual writing."

"And the clerk couldn't have done it because Mr. Ramsey read the will before and after," Pauline sighed. "Nothing makes sense. It had to have been Mr. Van Camp who wrote the will the way he did, but why? And what does it have to do with the stolen jewels? At first everything seemed to point to one of the beneficiaries. Now we have a jewel thief involved, and no clearer picture of the way the thief managed to stage manage the set. Every time I find another piece of information it makes things more cloudy, not less."

Something tugged at her brain, telling her she'd said something important, that somehow she'd laid her finger on the clue to the entire case ... but it was gone before she could focus on it.

"That's often the way it goes," James was saying. "It's like my mother's knitting after I would get into it when I was a shaver and tangle it. Every time I'd find an end and tug, thinking I could unravel the mess, the knots would get worse. But once Mother would get one knot undone, the rest almost always came loose of their own accord."

Pauline smiled ruefully. "I'm not much of a knitter, unfortunately. Do you have any analogies that are related to writing?"

"Now it's my turn to be sorry. I'm no hand at writing, and not even much of a reader. The papers and the occasional novel Ruby thinks I ought to try, that's it."

The papers ... it wasn't the clue she had given herself earlier, but something else clicked in Pauline's brain as she looked again at the list of names on James's desk.

Arabella Warren telling her she had been quoted in the *Watertown Daily Times* for her opinion on the end of Prohibition. David Anderson featured in a piece on the heroic loggers. Jane Casper's prize-winning cabbages mentioned in her local paper. Bertha Nelson's prize-winning quilt photographed for the *North Country Advance*.

"James!"

"What?"

"What old newspapers do you have here?"

"I don't know, why?"

"I think I know how Mr. X chose the heirs, or at least introduced their names to Mr. Van Camp—and it couldn't be Mr. Ramsey. I need all the newspapers for the Thousand Islands region, the *Times*, and, oh, just to prove my point, the *North Country Advance*."

"Mother takes that," James noted absently. "I can have the papers collected for you, but why?"

Pauline was already scribbling in her ubiquitous notepad. "I'll tell you in a minute. I need them for the dates around the time Mr. Van Camp's will was made."

Baffled but agreeable, James sent out for newspaper collection.

"What do you have in mind, Pauline?"

"Look," she said, showing him her notes. "Arabella *Warren*, mentioned in a piece in the *Watertown Daily Times*. Jane *Casper*, lives in Cape Vincent, mentioned in her local paper. Bertha *Nelson* in the *North Country Advance*. David *Anderson*, in the *Alexandria Bay News*, among others. And I remember that Arden Jamison was in the *Jefferson County Journal* recently. *Jamison*."

"I see what you're getting at," James said. "But—why? What's the point of it?"

"I don't know," Pauline said, frustrated. She had been so sure figuring out the origin of the heirs would be the key to solving the puzzle. "Let's confirm the theory first."

It took the rest of the morning, but they were eventually able to find Maria Thompson in the *Thousand Islands Sun* ("They even matched the 'Th,' that's dedication," James said); Richard Bracken in the *Black River Press*; Alan Caruthers in the *Carthage News*; Denis O'Leary in *On the St. Lawrence* ("Surely that should have been a paper starting with 'L'?" James asked, but Pauline insisted it was quite proper); Caroline Swanson in the *Sacketts Harbor Courier*; and Brian Nettleton in the *Northern New York Journal*.

"That's everyone except the Canadian fellow," James said, staring down at the neat list of names atop the scattered mounds of newspaper.

"How odd," Pauline said. "If you are matching surnames to newspaper names, and you are sticking with local papers, why suddenly jump to a Toronto man?"

James shrugged wearily. "Maybe it was a mistake."

"Maybe." Pauline was unconvinced.

"Or it could be that knot we need to undo in order to make everything else come clear," was James's next offering. "At the moment, I can't see which."

Pauline was weary as well, but her mind felt more clear than it had in days. At last they had something concrete. At last logic and scholarly elimination had gotten them somewhere.

"Thank you, James," she said, staggering to her feet—sitting for so long in one position checking the papers had left her horribly cramped.

"I'm not sure I did much," he said. "You're the one who made the connection between the papers and the people."

"I couldn't have done it if you hadn't jogged the idea in my brain."

"What's next for you?"

"Home," she said, savoring the thought. "I'm going to put the entire thing out of my mind for a time and see what else simmers to the surface."

Pauline suited deed to word, walking home in the crisp midday sun and then seating herself at the typewriter once back at Pleasant Street. She spent the rest of the day working on her current Emma Daring novel and typing up a piece on "The Mysterious Van Camp Heirs" to soothe a conscience still uneasy in stretching the truth to so many people in her initial investigation.

Arabella popped in that evening to let Pauline and Sarah know Mr. MacPhee had indeed confirmed the diamonds were paste, and that Jonathan was staying with her, "until we get answers to this riddle and nobody else is in danger."

"Another piece of the puzzle put in place, but the picture overall is still unclear," Pauline said. "Who took the jewels—who made the will—how could anyone do either of those without Mr. Van Camp and Mr. Ramsey knowing?"

"Or are we still looking at Mr. Ramsey as the villain?" Sarah asked hopefully.

"Maybe Mr. Van Camp really did do it all himself, even though Jonathan says it would be entirely out of character," Arabella said, plumping for her choice.

"Which do you think, Pauline? It had to be one of them."

"I think it's someone else entirely, but I don't know who, or how they did it," Pauline said.

"Mr. Gagne could have switched the jewels, and maybe he had a falling-out with his fellow thieves," Sarah mused. "That doesn't explain the will, nor Mr. Anderson's death, nor the attempted robbery. Who else could it be?"

"Who profits?" Pauline said. "That's the question Grandfather would ask, but in this case, it's only the jewel thief, and we've no way of knowing who that is."

"Or why he would go to the lengths of somehow convincing Mr. Van Camp to make a different will," Arabella said. "Wouldn't it have been easier to steal the jewels from Jonathan after he inherited them?"

"What about this Canadian? I want to know more about him," Sarah said. "He's a false note in the rest of this business, and I'd like to get him cleared away."

The three women were sharing a cup of chicory coffee around the kitchen table. Arabella had looked askance at Sarah at first, but was now talking with her as though she had never hesitated a moment.

"Oh!" said Pauline.

The other two looked at her.

"It was right there—everything—the whole solution, right at the back of my mind, and now it's gone. Just like this morning," she said, shaking her head in frustration.

"The important question is, what do we do now?" asked Arabella.

The question Pauline had brought to James at

the start of the day.

      She had no more idea now than she had then.

CHAPTER TWELVE

The Pinkerton Man

T he next thing that happened was not of Pauline's doing at all—at least, not directly. She was surprised at her typing the next day by a knock at the front door. She opened the door to reveal a stranger.

He was both tall and broad, straining at the seams of his navy suit, its shining silver buttons looking close to popping open. A bowler hat sat perched on the dark, slicked-back hair atop his head. His face was unshaven, and his small eyes were hard and dangerous. In one gloved hand he held a grimy envelope.

"Are you Pauline Gray?" he demanded as soon as the door opened, without even saying hello.

"I am," she replied. "Who are you?"

"Explain this to me," he said, thrusting the envelope forward and ignoring her question.

Pauline didn't need to look closely to recognize her own script addressing the envelope to Miller Horton, the lone Canadian amongst Mr. Van Camp's heirs. A prickle of undefined fear ran up her spine.

"Who are you?" she repeated.

"Ma'am, you need to tell me about this letter."

Pauline straightened her back and looked the man in the face, letting none of her nervousness show. "Either show me a badge or leave my home," she said quietly.

Heaving a great sigh, as though being asked to do something entirely unreasonable, the man dug into his pocket and flashed a small gold shield, replacing it too quickly for her to read the black lettering.

"Pinkerton's," he said. "Now answer the question."

Pauline frowned. "Why would private detectives be inquiring about a letter mailed to Canada? How did you even get a hold of it?"

"I am the one asking questions here, Miss Gray, and I suggest you start cooperating and answer them!" The man leaned forward, far too close to Pauline for comfort.

She refused to yield to his attempt at physical intimidation, despite the churning in her stomach that presaged an attack of nerves. "Step back, sir! I will answer no questions when they are accompanied by threats."

"What do you have to hide?" the man said, squinting his small eyes at her.

"I am beginning to wonder the same thing about you," Pauline replied. "If you are who you claim to be, and are here for legitimate purposes, you should have no objection to accompanying me to the police station and continuing this discussion there."

"Lady, I don't have time for your nonsense! You answer me right now, or—"

The altercation had drawn the attention of Pauline's landlady, who lived on the first floor of the two-story house. Her kitchen window flew open and she poked her head out and craned her neck to look up.

"Are you all right, Miss Gray? Do you need help? I see Kenny Mulgrew down the street, shall I call to him?" She pointed, and both Pauline and the Pinkerton man instinctively followed the direction of her finger.

Kenny Mulgrew was fourteen years old and the son and grandson of farmers; he already stood over six feet in his stocking feet and could throw feed bags of grain around like they were pillows.

The Pinkerton man snarled wordlessly, then brought himself under control.

"No trouble," he said. "We'll do this at the station. We'll see what your police have to say about you interfering with my duty."

"Thank you, Mrs. Harper," Pauline called down. "I think everything is fine for the moment."

Mrs. Harper continued to watch the detective even as Pauline closed the door in his face in order to put on her coat, hat, and gloves. Pauline's hands shook as she picked up her bag, but she couldn't tell if it was from fear or anger. How *dare* the man threaten her on her own doorstep! Thank heavens for valiant Mrs. Harper and dear Kenny.

Almost to the door, she paused, looking at her bag. She turned back to the bedroom, opened the nightstand drawer, and removed the unassuming pill-box. Something told her she might need its contents before the day was over.

The Pinkerton man had to precede Pauline down the outside staircase, it being too narrow to allow them to descend side-by-side or for him to move aside for her to go first. Once on the ground, he tried to take her arm, but Mrs. Harper cleared her throat from the kitchen window, and Pauline side-stepped him.

"We're going to the station now," she assured her landlady, and stepped out, setting such a brisk pace down the sidewalk that the bulky man was hard-pressed to keep up. Pauline's head was high and two spots of angry color flushed her usually pale cheeks. She was so angry her nausea had passed, though she knew it would return later, once this was over and done with.

The Pinkerton man was huffing and puffing by the time they reached the opera house.

He gaped at the stone building with its gothic windows and the towers on each of the four corners, and the bell tower in front. "This is your police station?" he gasped out, struggling to regain his breath as well as his former menacing mien.

Pauline opened the main door. "This is the Town Hall and Opera Theatre, the heart of our town —police included."

Young Officer Wallace was on duty at the station desk at the back of the opera house. His eyebrows raised nearly into his red hair at the sight of Pauline marching in trailed by a hulking, wheezing, scowling stranger.

"Is Lieutenant Richardson in?" Pauline inquired crisply.

"Y-yes ma'am," young Wallace said. "That way."

"Thank you," she said, walking past him and into James's office without stopping to knock.

That worthy officer of the law was tilted back in his chair behind his desk, studying some papers. At Pauline's entrance, he lost his balance, the chair crashing back down onto all fours, the papers scattering to every corner of the room.

"Tarnation! ... Pauline?"

"Lieutenant Richardson," she said formally, still furiously angry, "this man came to my home, demanded I answer his questions without identifying himself or his reason for asking, and threatened me —*in my own home*—if I did not capitulate to his demands."

"What?"

"Now then, miss, no need to be hysterical," the detective butted in. He had recovered enough of his breath and aplomb to step slightly in front of Pauline, forcing her to move aside or be trodden on, and smiled at James in a "we men against these foolish women" manner. "Frank Atkins, Pinkerton's Detective Agency." He handed his shield to James with far more courtesy than he had shown Pauline. "I admit, I was a bit brusque, but I didn't expect the lady to panic the way she did. A bit high-strung, isn't she?" He had the gall to chuckle. "I figured we'd step down here so the little miss felt safer. There was no real need to bother you, but—"

James shot to his feet. His face was dark red, his eyes narrowed and hard as flint. "You come into our town and question our citizens without having the courtesy to inform the police first? You threaten a lady of this town in her own home and then lie to my face about it? I will be telling my chief about this, and if he does not toss you in the lock-up overnight to teach you proper behavior I will be very surprised! This is outrageous!"

Atkins backpedaled rapidly. "No, no, it's all a misunderstanding! It's just a simple question! Nothing to bother the police with, just clearing up loose ends. It's a murder, you see, in Toronto. Last week, a man named Miller Norton. The police found this lady's letter at the scene and thought there was a chance she might have some information that could them catch his killer, so they contacted us and asked if we could investigate." He scowled. "We used to work for them regularly, until they developed their own investigative department, but they still use us for odd jobs and the like. Hardly worth my time, really."

James and Pauline exchanged a glance.

"The last Van Camp heir?" he asked her.

"The only one who wasn't in a local paper," she confirmed. "The odd man out."

"I'm getting the chief," he said.

"But—" the detective protested.

"This is a larger matter than you realize, as you would have learned had you come to us first," James said. "And we still need to deal with your treatment of Miss Gray."

"She exaggerated!" Atkins said. "She's a woman!"

"If there is one thing I've learned about Miss Gray over the last several years, it is that she never exaggerates," James said. "You, on the other hand, have already shown yourself to be prone to bluster and evasions. Of course I will believe her. And I fail to see what her being a woman has to do with any of this, except in that it makes your behavior even more egregious."

Atkins shot Pauline a glare of pure hatred as James called into the corridor for someone to fetch the chief, now. Pauline ignored it. He was of no concern to her, not now.

A third murder, the second heir to be killed, and the only one not connected to the papers. If she could, to use James's metaphor, unpick this one knot, she knew she could unravel the rest of it. The pieces were almost all in her hands; she only needed to put them together in the right positions.

Chief Gordon of Canton's Police Department heard James's succinct summation of the case thus far without comment, then withered Atkins with a glare when he heard how the man had come into town to question Pauline without first introducing himself and his needs to the force.

"I think we'd best bring in Miss Warren and the young Van Camp to fill out the details," he said as James wrapped up. "And have someone contact the police in the Thousand Islands. Technically speaking this seems to lie between them and the Toronto police, but since we've been brought into this matter to protect our own citizen from harassment, we'll coordinate matters from here. The letter from Miss Gray will be our justification, should we need it. We've been dragged into this, by gum we're going to see it wrapped up. I also need to contact the Chief Constable of the Toronto Police Department."

"Now look here!" Atkins said. "You can't just—"

"Do not," said Chief Gordon, "tell me what I can and cannot do."

For the next several hours, Pauline sat on a wooden chair in the corner of James's office and watched the activity.

From what Pauline could gather from James's end of the conversation, the police in the Thousand Islands continued to ridicule the notion of a connected conspiracy until he, sweating with fury, broke down their stubborn resistance point by point. Chief Gordon then took over James's desk to dictate a telegram to his Toronto counterpart informing him of the link between to cases. The telegram was short, to the point, and unmistakably angry over the breach in protocol by sending a Pinkerton man to Canton without informing the force.

When Arabella and Jonathan arrived, Pauline nodded a greeting to them but did not leave her corner. Arabella had matters well in hand, as her fluttery manner of speaking went away entirely when defending Jonathan Van Camp to the police.

"Thank you, Miss Warren," Chief Gordon said at last. "We don't necessarily suspect young Van Camp here, but we do have to ask these questions. I hope you understand."

"I do, sir," said Jonathan, who hovered as protectively over Arabella as she did him.

"I suppose to have to do your duty," Arabella graciously allowed.

All the while, Pauline mulled over the case, taking each seemingly disparate point and examining it, turning it around in her mind to look at it from a different angle to see if it might fit with the others from another perspective.

"Jonathan," she asked, "how many papers did your great-uncle read?"

"Only the *New York Times*," the young man answered. "He wasn't interested in local news."

Pauline nodded and added that fact to her musings.

"Richardson, where was Anderson killed?" she overheard Chief Gordon ask. "I'd like to know if we need to bring any other forces into this."

James checked the notes from the conversation with the Thousand Islands police. "Where is it, where is it, blast this wretched handwriting of mine, I can't read my own notes—there!" He looked up. "Utica."

Inability to read his own notes ... Utica ... the lost sapphire ...

Light began to glimmer.

"Mr. Atkins," Pauline said, turning to the sulky detective hunched in the opposite corner to hers. "What did you say this Miller's surname was?"

He ignored her.

"Answer the question, if you please," James bit out. "In this place, you will treat Miss Gray with respect."

"Norton," Atkins said, glaring at her. "You spelled in wrong in your letter. Not Horton—*Norton*."

That was it. That had to be it.

"And he was killed last week?"

"I already told you that, didn't you listen?"

"Was his head smashed in?"

"No," he said, pushing the words between his teeth. "He was poisoned."

"A woman's weapon," she said softly. "It all fits."

James looked over at her. "What?"

"I think I know who did it, how, and even why," she said.

"Oh, come now, Miss Gray," began Chief Gordon. "I don't deny you've been tremendously clever to collect all this information, but this is a matter for trained investigators now."

James coughed. "I think we ought to listen to her, sir. She's been right before. You remember the Ferris case last fall?"

"I just need proof," Pauline said. "Mr. Atkins, did Mr. Norton make a will?"

He mulishly clamped his mouth shut.

"Answer the lady's question, Atkins," Chief Gordon said, his mustache bristling with exasperation. However little he regarded Pauline's detective abilities, still less did he care for the Pinkerton man. "You've been warned once."

"Yes," Atkins ground out.

"Was his main beneficiary his brother?"

He stared. "How did you—"

"I need to see a copy of that will," Pauline said. "And I think we need to all take one last trip to Clayton for our final proof. Arabella and Jonathan included, and Sarah as well, for her medical knowledge. Each of them has contributed in one way or another to this case, and they need to be there for the wrapping up of it."

James looked at his chief, who looked at Pauline. She returned his gaze with quiet confidence.

"Very well, have it your way," Chief Gordon said, throwing up his hands in resignation. "Somebody ring them up and tell them to prepare for us."

CHAPTER THIRTEEN

Truth Revealed

They were all squeezed into the lawyer's office in Clayton—Mr. Atkins holding himself as aloof as possible from the rest; Arabella standing next to Jonathan Van Camp; Sarah in her nurse's uniform, having had no time to change between leaving the hospital and joining the rest of them; Mrs. David Anderson, looking tired but determined, a glimmer of hope at the back of her eyes; James and Chief Gordon with their thumbs hooked in their pockets, waiting for the proof of the murderer's identity; two Thousand Islands police officers scowling at the rest of them; and finally, Mr. Ramsey and his staff.

"Er—I appreciate that you are all here, I suppose, but it is a bit, er, unconventional, isn't it?" Mr. Ramsey said. "Shouldn't you police just arrest the murderer and thief and tell us all about it afterward?" He glared at Jonathan as he said "murderer and thief."

The young man stared defiantly back. "I for one want to have it all out in the open," he said.

"There is such a tangle of information and misinformation in this case that it seems impossible to sort it all and prove the murderer without going through it all step by step, with everyone contributing his or her piece of the puzzle," James said gravely.

Pauline approved the way he phrased it.

"Miss Gray here has assembled most of the framework herself, which is why we will now be turning this over to her," Chief Gordon added. "Miss Gray?"

So many eyes on her, some hostile, some confused, some hopeful, a few confident. Pauline's stomach twisted. If she should be wrong ...!

But she wasn't. This was the only thing that made sense.

"The question at the heart of this case has always been: why did Mr. Van Camp make such a strange will? Mr. Ramsey here suggested it was a philanthropic gesture and a way of showing his displeasure with his great-nephew. Others have thought it the quixotic whim of an old man. Miss Warren considered it an act of benevolence toward his great-nephew, once we learned the jewels were fake. I believe it was none of these things. I am convinced that the will we have all accepted as Mr. Van Camp's is a fake."

Mr. Ramsey burst into speech before anyone else. "Now look here, young lady, that is a serious accusation, very serious indeed! How dare you suggest —"

Pauline held up a hand. "Please let me finish." There was a crack of authority in her voice that surprised the lawyer into silence.

"I discovered recently that each heir but one had been chosen based on their name appearing in a newspaper that shared the same first initial—for example, Arabella Warren in the *Watertown Daily Times*. Mr. Van Camp, we have learned, did not read any of the local newspapers.

"The will had been witnessed by two men: Jasper Randolph, the gardener; and Mr. Gagne, the butler-*cum*-valet. Mr. Randolph was gotten out of the country by a mysterious gift he assumed to be from his former employer, and Mr. Gagne was murdered."

"Mr. Gagne's death was declared an accident," spoke up one of the Clayton policemen.

"Yes," said Pauline. "That was a mistake on your part."

He sputtered indignantly, but let her continue.

"The next to die was Miller Norton, a man living in Toronto, Canada, who inherited Mr. Van Camp's small but priceless art collection—the only beneficiary not named in a local newspaper, and the only one to receive art instead of jewelry."

"Horton, you mean," broke in Mr. Ramsey.

"His name was written as Horton on the list you gave Miss Warren, but that was another lie," Pauline said. "Mr. Atkins?"

"It was Norton, sure enough," he growled.

"But that's—" Mr. Ramsey began.

"The next death was that of David Anderson," Pauline said loudly, overriding whatever the lawyer had been going to say. "A good man and loving father, who so questioned the authenticity of the inheritance he received that he asked a jeweler to examine the earrings, and in so doing lost his life. The jewels proved to be as false as the will that directed their disposal."

"Our apologies for the difficult topic, ma'am," said the other Clayton policeman to Mrs. Anderson, shooting a poisonous glare at Pauline.

Mrs. Anderson intercepted the glare and directed it back toward him. "Don't apologize for the topic, apologize for letting this happen! At least Miss Gray is doing something toward catching my husband's murderer."

Pauline coughed, touched and embarrassed by the woman's confidence.

"At first, Sarah—Miss Jones, that is—and I suspected Mr. Ramsey of being our villain. He was the lawyer who made Mr. Van Camp's will; he easily could have altered it. He had the jewelry in his safe, making it simple for him to switch the stones. He was even in Utica at the time Mr. Anderson was murdered. He could have done all of this so he could sell the real jewels and reap his dishonest reward."

"Well, of all the—" spluttered Mr. Ramsey.

"We were wrong," Pauline said.

"I should think so!" exclaimed the lawyer.

"How can you be sure, Pauline?" asked James.

She directed her words toward him while watching the lawyer out of the corner of her eye.

"Because Mr. Ramsey is losing his vision. He can no longer read."

The lawyer's face turned white. His legs gave

out, and he clutched at the desk for support.

"I suspect cataracts," she continued. "He mistook my white blouse for yellow the other day, which Miss Jones informs me is a common symptom of cataracts. And while this reception area is a painfully bright white, even to non-diseased eyes, his office is so dimly lit as to make reading anything nearly impossible. Finally, he admitted that he does not read the papers anymore. He passed it off as though he does not have the time, but the excuse rang false from the first. A lawyer who does not enjoy the morning paper over breakfast? Highly implausible.

"Mr. Ramsey claimed he glanced over the list of bequests before handing it over to his clerk to write out properly, but in reality he relied on the clerk to do the reading for him, just as he relies on his secretary to tell him any news of importance in the papers."

Sarah stepped forward to peer at Mr. Ramsey's face. "I do see the beginning of cloudiness," she said. "It's the early stages of cataracts."

He put up a hand to shield his eyes. "How can *you* possibly know that, young woman?"

"I am a nurse," she reminded him. "Why hide it? You can have surgery to remove cataracts. There's no shame in it."

He straightened angrily. "No shame! Who would want a lawyer who is going blind, who has to rely on his clerk and secretary to do all his reading? Nobody would ever trust me again. And don't talk to me about surgery—Eleanor researched all that when my vision first started clouding over and told me that most of the time the surgery leaves the patient worse off than before. No, no surgery for me!" He looked around, his anger turned now to pleading.

"I shouldn't have hidden the truth, I know, but I was too afraid of losing my clients! Eleanor and George said they would act as my eyes, and I thought, well, I would just keep going as long as I could. There's no crime in that!"

"But if he didn't read the list of bequests, or write the will, or even read the newspapers, that means..." Arabella began.

"He couldn't have chosen the heirs," Sarah finished, stepping away from the lawyer with sadness on her face.

"Exactly," Pauline nodded.

"And if the clerk wrote the will, that means—" James said, waiting by the door with a deceptively casual stance.

"Yes," agreed Pauline. "That means our true villains are the pair who kept their employer's secret and used it for their own gain."

George and Miss Peck had been modestly effacing themselves at the back of the office while this was going on. At Pauline's announcement of Mr. Ramsey's eye troubles, they had exchanged uneasy glances and started slithering toward the door.

James and Chief Gordon blocked their way.

"Mr. Ramsey told me of George Norton's unsatisfactory brother who had been shipped off to Canada after he disgraced the family. It's not that much of a stretch to guess his name was Miller. Mr. Ramsey never made the connection between the Miller Horton list of heirs and Miller Norton, George's brother, because George never told him the man's first name, only the surname, and that was changed just enough to not ring any bells."

"You can't prove that," George spoke up at last. Everyone had instinctively drawn apart from the pair, leaving a clear space around them. Mrs. Anderson had recoiled almost to the opposite wall, eyes burning in her white face. Pauline couldn't bear to look at her for long.

"Mr. Atkins?" Pauline said.

The Pinkerton man seemed at last to have forgiven her for being a woman and unintimidated by him. The more uncomfortable Mr. Ramsey and his staff became, the more he seemed to be enjoying himself. "Miller Norton in his will left everything of which he was possessed to his brother George Norton."

Pauline broke the silence that filled the room at that pronouncement. "So you see it all starts to come together. George Norton and Eleanor Peck saw their opportunity when Mr. Ramsey was called out to the Van Camp place to make a will. Mr. Van Camp was well-known locally for his jewelry collection and ownership of three Moillon paintings. George of course accompanied Mr. Ramsey, secretly carrying with him a second will form and a pre-written list of names culled from various newspapers. He wrote out the will as Mr. Van Camp intended, and then, while Mr. Van Camp was showing Mr. Ramsey the jewelry, George filled in the second will and changed the bequests intended for Jonathan to the names on his list. Mr. Van Camp saw the will he intended, but the will that was signed and witnessed was the false one. George even had a ready-made excuse, covering up the will for the witnesses to sign as is proper. Mr. Ramsey, unable to read the original will, never knew its contents, and so assumed everything was in order."

Jonathan made a quick movement toward George Norton. "You thieving, lying—"

Arabella grabbed his arm and hauled him back. "Let her finish," she said. "Leave him to the police."

"Worse was to come," Pauline said. "As soon as Mr. Van Camp died and the will passed probate, Miss Peck left for Toronto, where she murdered Mr. Miller Norton so the paintings would come to George."

A cry broke from Mr. Ramsey's throat. "No! Not Eleanor! She wouldn't betray me like that."

"I'm afraid she did," Pauline said. "In fact, I strongly suspect she was the driving force behind the entire plot. Her lies to you about cataract surgery mean she's been planning something of this sort for a long time."

"Lies?"

"Cataract surgery is dangerous, as is any surgery, Mr. Ramsey, but nowhere near so bad as Miss Peck told you," Sarah said in a gentle voice.

Mr. Ramsey groaned and buried his face in his hands.

Pauline cleared her throat, glancing around the room. Chief Gordon and James were nodding along as she spoke, their attention divided between listening to her and making sure Miss Peck and George didn't make a break for the door. Jonathan continued to glare at George, while Arabella was clearly more concerned with him than with the revelations. Mrs. Anderson—Pauline moved on. Even the Thousand Islands police seemed to believe her now.

"Mr. Ramsey mentioned to me that Miss Peck has a cousin who is a jeweler. I believe she was the one who first thought of switching the jewels; George, the art lover, would likely have been content with adding his brother onto the real will so as to get his hands on the paintings once Miller's debauched lifestyle led to his inevitably early demise."

She had no proof of that, but judging by their personalities she was confident in her assertion. George had struck her all along as weak, whereas Miss Peck was both ruthless and amoral.

George was pale and sweating now, but Miss Peck watched the entire proceeding with aloof disdain, standing somewhat apart from him. Only her fingers, fiddling with the clasp on her handbag, gave away a hint of nerves.

"What about poor old Mr. Gagne?" Jonathan asked.

"I can't be entirely certain, but I suspect he discovered the fraud. Perhaps he saw George changing the bequests, or maybe George dropped the list of names and Mr. Gagne picked it up without realizing at first what it signified. They sent Jasper Randolph away to stop him from gossiping or suspecting anything was amiss, but they couldn't leave the property without a caretaker. When he realized what they were up to, they tried to bribe him with the sapphires taken from Mr. Anderson's earrings. He wouldn't take them, and so George, presumably, lost his temper and hit him over the head with a rock, killing Mr. Gagne and losing one of the sapphires in the process. He left one of Mr. Ramsey's distinctive red handkerchiefs by the body, either by accident or as yet another way to distract attention from the real culprits." She stopped and swallowed, the picture she was painting with her words almost too vivid for her own self.

"And my David?" asked Mrs. Anderson, her voice hoarse.

"They didn't want anyone to figure out the jewels were false. Their one hope was for everything to settle down and for nobody to ask too many questions. Arabella Warren was the first to put a spoke in their plans by asking me to investigate. Your husband, Mrs. Anderson, was another complication. They hoped by killing him and taking the earrings they could make it appear he had been murdered for the gems, proving they were valuable. They didn't count on his wife being privy to his plans and seeing the discrepancies in the setup."

"If David Anderson was killed in Utica, how did they do that?" Chief Gordon asked. He kept a wary eye on George Norton, who looked almost ready to bolt despite the officers blocking the doorway.

"You remember I said Mr. Ramsey was in Utica the same night? Miss Peck and George were with him.

They even met Mr. Anderson earlier in the day, which is when he told them of his intentions to have the earrings evaluated. After the meeting of the Bar Association finished and Mr. Ramsey retired for the night, George tracked down David Anderson and killed him. I'm sorry, Mrs. Anderson."

The woman nodded, her face tight.

"By now the conspirators were getting extremely nervous. Nothing was going according to plan. The earrings had been evaluated before Mr. Anderson was killed, and the information shared with others. In an attempt to both shift suspicion back onto Mr. Van Camp's great-nephew and persuade people the jewelry was worth something, they attempted to rob Arabella. Not only did the robbery fail, Jonathan stopped George, the would-be-thief, and so simply *could not* have been the robber."

"I should think not!" said Arabella, stretching up to put a protective arm around the boy's shoulders. He gave her a startled glance, and then smiled.

"Now for the final proof," Pauline said. "Mr. Ramsey, you mentioned the other day that George had sent some of his paintings off to be framed and he was expecting them returned any day now. They were coming to the office because he didn't trust such valuable items to be sent to his boarding house. I presume those are them?" She nodded to the brown paper-wrapped rectangles leaning against the wall in the back.

"No!" shouted George, lunging forward.

All was chaos for a few moments as James wrestled George into submission and the Clayton police tore the paper off the parcels, revealing three exquisite Baroque paintings.

"Those are Great-Uncle Horace's all right," Jonathan said. "He had them hanging in the dining room, where I saw them every week at dinner. I'd recognize them anywhere."

"You still have no proof I was involved in any of this." Miss Peck chose now to speak, casting a disdainful eye at the writhing George. "I have a cousin who is a jeweler and I happened to be out of town at the time George's brother was poisoned. What of it?"

"Oh no," snarled George, still struggling in James's grip. "I'm not going down alone. The entire thing was your plan, from start to finish! I only thought of defrauding the old man of the paintings and waiting for my brother to die—he drank too much and lived too rough a life, I knew I wouldn't have long to wait. The jewels and the murders were your idea. The whole reason you told Ramsey not to have surgery was so you could use him to cheat people." He stopped struggling and turned his head to look at James. "Van Camp was the first, but she had just been waiting for her chance. I helped, but she was the one behind it. I'll confess everything if it means she gets arrested too!"

Before anyone could move, Eleanor Peck whipped a tiny pistol out of her handbag, pointed it at George Norton, and calmly pulled the trigger. A shot cracked. Arabella and Mrs. Anderson screamed.

James let go of George, stumbled back, and

clutched his bleeding arm where the bullet had nicked him. George slumped to the floor, blood flowing copiously from the wound in his chest. Sarah dashed forward to tend him.

Chief Gordon and the other policemen lunged toward Miss Peck, but halted when she turned the pistol on Mr. Ramsey.

"If anyone takes one more step, I will shoot him as well," she said. She smiled contemptuously when everyone froze in place.

"I thought at first I should shoot you, Miss Gray, but you would never have put it all together if Ramsey hadn't talked so much. Oh yes, you're very clever, it took so much effort to put the pieces together with this fool dropping clues right and left, dangling the truth in front of your very nose. I will give you credit at least for figuring out how and why Gagne died. You pieced it together nicely, I admit. It was the list of names he picked up after George dropped them, like a clumsy idiot. And then George had to go and lose his nerve when Gagne refused the bribe, flinging away the sapphire. Hit him over the head with a rock and bolted. I had to go back once he'd told me what he'd done and set the scene to look like an accident, and it took me so long to find the list from where it had blown that I didn't have time to search for the sapphire. I was the one who left the handkerchief, Miss Gray. I hoped that if the police did think it murder, they would assume that Mr. Ramsey had conspired with the butler to steal the jewels and then killed him. I wish they had.

"George was bad enough, but worst of all was you, Alan Ramsey. You never stop talking. Never! After all these years, you never notice George or me as anything more than your cover for your shameful secret and your audience for your endless babbling. We pulled this off right under your nose and you were too busy chattering to see it."

"Put the gun down and let's talk this over," said Chief Gordon in a strained voice. "You've already killed one man, maybe two. You don't want another death on your conscience."

"If I had a conscience, I suppose I wouldn't," said Miss Peck indifferently. "Then again, after two deaths, what's one more? But in fact, I don't particularly care. I am walking out that door, and if anyone tries to stop me, I am shooting Alan Ramsey."

"Oh no you aren't," snarled Jonathan, and he threw himself at Miss Peck. Pauline, body reacting before her brain engaged, swept to the side and pulled Mr. Ramsey with her out of the line of fire.

The gun went off—Arabella cried out again— blood poured from Jonathan's arm but he had his hands on the gun now, wrestling it aside—the police recovered from their stupefaction and moved in to help—it was over. Eleanor Peck was disarmed and in handcuffs.

Her face showed no more emotion than it had at any time Pauline had seen it.

Sarah rose to her feet from her examination of George Norton.

"He'll live," she said. "But he needs to be in a

hospital. James, Jonathan, I'll need to look at both your arms and get bandages on them."

"And then," Arabella burst out, the speech pouring forth as though she couldn't hold it in a moment longer, "you're coming home with me for good, Jonathan Van Camp. You and I, we both need a family. I don't care about any diamond necklace, paste or real. I want you to live with me as my son, and you'll never have to worry about a home again. You can even bring your half-sisters to live with us if you think your stepfather will let them go. My house is large enough for you all."

Jonathan had endured the gunshot wound without a whimper, but at that his composure finally cracked. "Oh," he said faintly.

Pauline turned away so she wouldn't have to see his tears.

The police took the two conspirators away, George on a makeshift stretcher with Sarah close beside, checking his pulse. Mr. Atkins followed glumly behind. The case was solved, but he would get no glory from it.

Chief Gordon nodded to Pauline on his way out. "Seems Lieutenant Richardson was right about you. Well done, Miss Gray."

That left Mr. Ramsey and Mrs. Anderson. The lawyer, shaken and defeated, Pauline could do nothing about. In a way, Miss Peck had been right. His deception and self-absorption had allowed this to happen. There was no shame in losing his eyesight, but to lie about it and use others to fulfill his responsibilities, violating his clients' privacy in the process, was appalling. Even if Miss Peck had lied to him and played upon his fears, Pauline could not excuse him entirely.

The actions of his employees were not his fault, but he had to bear the responsibility for his own deeds.

The widow was another matter.

"I wish I could give you a happy ending," Pauline said.

"At least you gave me justice," Mrs. Anderson answered.

"I know this won't restore him, or make up for his being gone, but I have something here that belongs to you," Pauline said.

She hadn't discussed this with Jonathan, but she was confident he would follow her lead. Pauline pulled the blue sapphire out of her handbag. She opened her hand to reveal it to Mrs. Anderson.

The other woman gasped. "That's—the real stone!"

"One of them, anyway."

"But I can't take that. The will was fake."

Pauline glanced over her shoulder. Jonathan had recovered enough from his shock at Arabella's offer to take notice of his surroundings again. He stepped forward.

"It will take the lawyers—proper lawyers," with a glower at poor, broken Mr. Ramsey, "years to figure out who legally gets what, even if they ever manage to recover the rest of the stolen jewels. Miss

Warren was right. She and I both need a family more than anything. That's the best legacy my great-uncle could have left me. I think he would have wanted you to have the sapphire, as our family's apology for what was done to you. Please accept it with our respect and sorrow."

Arabella had good instincts. Jonathan Van Camp was proving himself a fine young man already.

"I still feel I ought not," said Mrs. Anderson. "But my children have to eat. Thank you."

She gingerly took the sparkling blue gem from Pauline's hand.

A weight lifted off Pauline's shoulders as the widow closed her fingers around the stone, nodded a farewell to them, and hurried out. It was not enough, but it was something.

Two murderers unmasked, two lonely people given a family, and a widow provided for. It would not bring the dead back to life, nor magically untangle the complications of the falsified will, nor make up Mr. Ramsey's loss. In an imperfect world, justice could never be perfectly accomplished.

Nevertheless, Pauline had done what she could. The rest, she would leave to a higher power.

"Come," she said, looking at her friends. "It's time to go home."

The End

AMAZON EDITION

Cover design by Louise Bates

StarDance Press
stardancepress.com

ABOUT THE AUTHOR

Louise Bates

 Louise Bates is the alter ego of fantasy/sci-fi author E.L. Bates. She lives on the New England coast with her husband and children, and when she is not writing can usually be found reading, knitting, or exploring the shore.

THE PAULINE GRAY NOVELLAS

Candles In The Dark

Diamonds To Dust

Secrets Of The Past

Coming soon